THE THIRD
BEAR HUG

THE THIRD BEAR HUG

James D. Navratil

To order additional copies of this book, contact:
Xlibris
1-888-795-4274
www.Xlibris.com
Orders@Xlibris.com
814050

Contents

Synopsis of *The Bear Hug* by Sylvia Tascher

The Third Bear Hug is a continuation of the stories in *The Bear Hug* and *The Final Bear Hug*. The following is a summary of the first book.

The prologue of *The Bear Hug* begins at the new headquarters of the International Atomic Energy Agency (IAEA) in Vienna, where Margrit Czermak is copying for a Russian agent confidential documents belonging to her husband, Dr. John James Czermak, a world-renowned nuclear scientist and contributor to the development of the neutron bomb. Subsequently, the Russian Security (KGB) agent sexually attacks Margrit, and as she is fleeing, her lover, Andrei Pushkin, intervenes and is shot by the agent.

In chapter 3, a red Mercedes-Benz roadster is seen inching its way around the Gurtel (Vienna's outer perimeter street), the driver eyeing the few scantily clad prostitutes who are soliciting their wares despite the heavy snow that had blanketed the city. We then proceed with him to the third district, where a Ukrainian dance ensemble, sponsored by the United Nations' (UN) Russian Club of Art and Literature, had just finished its performance. During the cocktail party that followed, Andrei Pushkin, suspected by the U.S. Central Intelligence Agency (CIA) of being a covert Russian agent, captivated by a woman's melodious laugh, turned to gaze in her direction. He was immediately enraptured by the beautiful, charming Margrit Czermak gracing the arm of Boris Mikhailov, a prominent man with the IAEA, as he steered her in the direction of her husband. Meanwhile, two covert agents of the KGB, huddled in the background, are discussing the instructions received from the Kremlin to elicit from the prominent American scientist his knowledge of the neutron bomb, by whatever means necessary.

A few months later, on Margrit's return flight from London, where she had been attending her stricken brother, she encountered and was consoled by the compassionate Pushkin. In due course, he invited her to dine with him. As her husband's travel had again necessitated his prolonged absence from the city, in a state of extreme loneliness, she accepted Andrei's invitation.

In the interim, both the KGB and the CIA kept the American woman under surveillance, it being the KGB's intention to instigate an illicit relationship and the CIA's to use her to entrap Pushkin.

At the same time, John Czermak was suffering profound personal problems. While he had been employed in the nuclear weapons field in Colorado, his scientific endeavors had demanded first priority. As his present position with the IAEA had created substantial leisure time, he was both angered and dismayed to realize his wife's newly found independence. And being a man of high moral values, it never occurred to him that his wife was to become romantically involved with another man. To compound matters, he had belatedly sought to create an atmosphere of congeniality with his children, only to discover that he had little rapport with them.

With the passing of time, the clandestine liaison between the American and Russian flourished, eventually culminating in Paris and again in the Soviet capitol. However, realizing the futility of their relationship, they had on several occasions unsuccessfully attempted to terminate it. Meanwhile, the KGB, eager to record on film the boudoir events of the couple, applied pressure to Andrei by kidnapping his younger son. Thus, successful in obtaining the desired photographs, they were able to prevail upon Margrit for information relevant to her husband's work at the Colorado nuclear facility. During an assignation, a CIA agent met his death as he was propelled in front of a high-speed subway train. As Margrit had witnessed the event, an attempt was then made to eliminate her as well.

The relationship with her husband continued to deteriorate, and John made good his threats to leave her. Therefore, she beseeched Andrei to abandon his family to share a life with her. But Andrei had undergone a substantial ideological transformation during his affair with Margrit and, as a result, suffered continual agonizing self-debasement. Thus, he eventually took his own life.

Shocked beyond belief by the receipt of her lover's farewell letter, Margrit deliberated between life and death. Her friend, the Austrian Anna Winkler, who minutes before had heard of Andrei's suicide on the midmorning news broadcast, drove frantically to reach Margrit in time. And John, unaware of the morning's bizarre events but certain he wanted his beloved wife at any cost, rushed to make amends to her from the opposite side of the city.

Synopsis of *The Final Bear Hug* by James D. Navratil and Sylvia Tascher

The Final Bear Hug is a continuation of the story in *The Bear Hug*. The story begins with John James Czermak and his wife, Margrit, returning to their home in Arvada, Colorado, after spending almost three years in Vienna, Austria, where John worked for the IAEA. John is a world-renowned nuclear scientist and contributor to the development of the controversial neutron bomb. He returns to the job as manager of Plutonium Chemistry Research and Development at the Rocky Flats Plant (RFP), where triggers for nuclear weapons are made. In Vienna, Margrit was romantically involved with Andrei Pushkin, thought by the CIA to be a KGB agent. Realizing the futility of their relationship, Andrei and Margrit had on several occasions unsuccessfully attempted to terminate it. But Andrei suffered continual agonizing self-debasement and eventually left Vienna for Canada after faking his suicide.

Following their return to Colorado, John and Margrit resumed a close, loving relationship that had been damaged in Vienna. About this time, John was recruited by Tim Smith of the CIA since John traveled to conferences around the world and to Vienna and Moscow to have meetings with his Russian coauthors on a series of books they were writing for the IAEA. Following more contacts with his Russian colleagues, John was informed that a background investigation had been conducted by the Department of Energy (DOE) and the FBI. This investigation resulted in John losing his security clearance.

John was then granted a three-year leave of absence from Rocky Flats management to teach in Australia. Tim continued to keep in contact with John and asked him to visit certain countries and find out if they might be producing nuclear weapons. During his travels, there were several attempts on his life. After his return from his leave of absence in Australia, John started work in California. It was there that Andrei surprisingly contacted Margrit, trying to renew their love affair. Margrit rejected him since she had a good relationship with John and told Andrei she might go with him if she was a divorcée or a widow. This statement prompted Andrei to try and kill John, but instead, he accidently killed Margrit. Back at his home in Canada, he learned of her death and committed suicide. In his dying breath, he told his son, Alex, that John had shot him.

John wanted to start a new life and left California for a teaching job at Clemson University in South Carolina and even started using his middle name. Andrei's son, Alex, joined James's research group using a different last name. The story concluded during an expedition in Antarctica that Tim supported to see if one of the Russian crew members was passing nuclear weapons information to a group of Argentinian scientists. On the expedition, Alex tried to kill James but later found out that James did not kill his father. On the last night of the voyage, he met James at the stern of the ship and made amends to him, which ended by Alex giving James a big bear hug that caused both of them to accidentally fall into the rough and freezing ocean.

Prologue

Clemson University, located in the upstate of South Carolina, is a land-grant institution founded in 1889. The 1,400-acre campus is near the foothills of the Blue Ridge Mountains and sits next to Lake Hartwell, a 17,500-acre Clemson Experimental Forest, and the towns of Clemson and Pendleton. The forest is used for education, research, and recreation. This public university is the second-largest one in South Carolina with more than twenty-five thousand undergraduate and graduate students.

Not far from the home of Clemson University's president, about the middle of campus, is the four-story Hunter Chemistry Building. The first floor contains general chemistry laboratories, the second floor some teaching and administrative rooms, the third a mix of teaching and research laboratories, and the top floor mostly research laboratories. Prof. John James Czermak, chairman of the chemistry department, has his office and research laboratory on the fourth floor.

The six-foot Czermak had been told many times that he resembles the Hollywood actor Tom Cruise. Indeed, his resemblance to Mr. Cruise is striking. And it is these handsome features, together with enticing azure blue eyes and lustrous black hair, extraordinary physique, and an undeniable aura of machismo, that bring stares from women of all ages.

On a Saturday night, it is unusual to find anyone in the chemistry building, especially since it is a rainy and windy evening. Earlier, Czermak had been showing his graduate student Igor Medvedev how to operate the gas chromatograph/mass spectrometer systems. Now he is performing another experiment with the instrument. As the apparatus spews forth its analysis onto a stream of graph paper, Czermak grasps the paper with one hand to study the pattern developing. He runs his other hand through his thick black hair, a boyhood habit. So engrossed is he with the analysis, he is unaware that behind him, the laboratory door has opened. An unseen hand tosses a Molotov cocktail into the room, which explodes at once, shooting flames in every direction. Czermak springs to his feet. His unbelieving eyes race about to see chemical after chemical explode and wonders why the sprinkler system is not operating. The sea of flames creates an inferno, and within seconds, fire is licking at James's feet and legs. Poisonous fumes have permeated the air, choking, blinding, and disorienting him. It does not occur to him that fire extinguishers are located on each side of the door.

As he is crawling across the laboratory floor, he is thinking not only about saving his life but also how his wife recently got burned alive after a hit-and-run driver smashed into his convertible, turning it over and bursting in flame. He knew it was no accident and that the crash was meant for him as Ying always drove her own car to work in the chemistry building.

Chapter 1
Chile

I

Cape Horn, located on the small island of Hornos, is the most southern part of Chile. It is where the Pacific and Atlantic Oceans meet. This area is very hazardous because of strong currents, high winds, and large waves, making it dangerous for ships transporting goods around the world prior to the building of the Panama Canal. Today cruise ships, yachts, and small sailing vessels use the channels north of the cape, between Wollaston and Hermite Islands or between Tierra el Fuego and Isla Navarino, to avoid the dangerous seas around the cape.

Puerto Williams, located in the middle of the north side of Navarino Island, faces the Beagle Channel and is the most southerly city in the world. It is located 240 miles south of Punta Arenas, 100 miles from Cape Horn, and almost 500 miles from Antarctica. Settlements have existed there since the nineteenth century. Puerto Williams was founded in 1953 and was established initially as a base of the Chilean Navy. Now it has approximately three thousand inhabitants, half of which are nonnaval citizens who work in artistry, commerce, fisheries, public administration, scientific research, schools, tourism, and shops. The city has an airport, fire and police stations, several hostels and bed-and-breakfasts, four restaurants, two small supermarkets, two bars, a bakery, two churches, a museum, a tourist agency, a kindergarten, an all-grades school, a university center, and a naval hospital. Navarino Island is mostly covered by beautiful mountains and has one of the densest concentrations of archeological sites in the world. The island attracts tourists for its aquatic birds, botany, fishing, geology, hiking, and mountain climbing.

An unpaved fourteen-mile road that parallels the Beagle Channel leaves Puerto Williams to the east and ends at Puerto Eugenia. One occupied farm is located there as well as the beginning of a hiking trail that ends in Puerto Toro, where some fishing boats dock for king crab catching. In going west out of Puerto Williams, the thirty-two-mile unpaved road ends at Puerto Navarino, where a hiking trail to Caleta Wulaia begins. There is a ferry that travels between Ushuaia and Puerto Navarino, a shorter route than between Puerto Williams and Ushuaia. There were many occupied homes along this road in the past, but the homeowners moved to Puerto Williams. Now there are only two occupied farms near Puerto Navarino.

One of the farms near Puerto Navarino is owned by a retired medical doctor, Deborah Klose. She and her husband worked at the naval hospital in Puerto Williams until his heart attack and death a year ago. Thus, she retired early and sold her house in Puerto Williams because the wonderful memories with her husband haunted her. Then she moved to their weekend home. She enjoys the remote and quiet life, living off farming, ranching, and fishing.

Her nearest neighbors, Eduardo and his wife, Maria, have about the same size farm as Deborah, ten acres. Eduardo took care of the Kloses' ranch during their absence. Eduardo's farm has a dock for his small fishing boat. The thirty-foot wooden fishing boat has a cabin for the pilot as well as a sleeping area. The area behind the cabin is large enough for his *Zodiac*, and under deck are storage areas and another small sleeping area. He mainly uses the boat for fishing and travels to other towns and islands. Both farms have vegetable gardens in greenhouses and fruit trees as well as a few chickens, cows, goats, and sheep.

Early one morning, following a violent rain and windstorm, the threesome went to the small island of Hornos in Eduardo's boat to do some fishing. At one point, they spotted a man lying on the beach. They then took the *Zodiac* to shore to discover the man asleep. He looked awfully bad with bruises and cuts on his face and hands. They immediately covered the man with a coat as he awoke. Deborah asked him in both Spanish and English, "Are you okay?"

He replied in American English, "Yes, I am okay, but very tired, thirsty, and cold."

She then asked him, "What is your name, and how did you get washed up on shore?"

"I do not know."

Eduardo stated, "A cruise ship went by in the middle of the night heading for Antarctica, and he must have fallen off the ship."

Deborah said, "Let us put him in the *Zodiac*, where I can bandage him up and give him some water. Although it will take us the rest of the day, we need to take him to my home for recovery."

Once at Deborah's farm, she gave the injured man more water and properly bandaged him up. Deborah then asked Eduardo to put him in one of her two bedrooms to get some sleep. The home also has a spacious living room, kitchen, dining room, and bathrooms in each bedroom. From the front covered porch, one has an excellent view of the channel and forest.

II

Late the next day, after the stranger was rested and had a shower, Deborah invited him to come to dinner. She had given him one of her husband's robes to wear. Over a meal of fish, corn, and salad, she asked him again, "Who are you, and how did you get here?"

"I do not know, but I am still very tired."

"Please go to the bedroom and sleep as long as you want. You can also use any of my late husband's clothes that I moved from my bedroom."

About twenty-four hours later, the rescued man, dressed in a fresh set of the clothes of Deborah's late husband, met her in the dining room for another dinner. Over dinner, they talked in both English and Spanish. Deborah thought that he must have learned Spanish from a teacher from Spain. She told him about herself.

"My name is Deborah, but you can call me Deb. I grew up in Santiago, and am a widow and medical doctor. I took early retirement from working at the naval hospital in Puerto Williams after my husband died a year ago from a heart attack, probably caused by his long hours at the hospital. I met my husband when we were in medical school at the University of Santiago. Then we did our internship at the naval hospital in Puerto Williams and continued working there."

He thanked her for taking such good care of him as he thought what a beautiful, kind, caring, and intelligent lady she was and about his age.

Deborah continued. "You look a lot like my late husband, Richard. We did not have any children or siblings, and our parents have gone to heaven. We inherited this weekend home from Richard's father. His father was the head doctor at the naval hospital, and Richard replaced him when he passed. His mother had died five years earlier in an accident. Eduardo lives in the adjoining farm with his beautiful wife, Maria. She was the one that helped me and Eduardo bring you here. Eduardo assists me around the farm. I pay him well since I have my husband's life insurance money, our savings, money from selling our big home in town, and my retirement income. All three of us are mostly self-sufficient, growing vegetables and fruit, caring for the animals and fishing. We also go on lots of hikes, and I read a lot, especially murder mysteries. We rarely must leave the farms for shopping. When we must shop, Eduardo takes Maria and I in his fishing boat to Ushuaia, Argentina, although we could drive to Puerto Williams, but it takes longer. The road is muddy after rainstorms, but the snow is plowed in the winter. I also have a piano that I play, and I usually sing. Since we have finished our meal, let me play and sing my favorite song, 'The Way We Were,' by Barbara Streisand."

III

Days later, as the injured man continued to recover, Deborah told him, "You are welcome to stay as long as you like, especially since you do not know where your home is. You can help Eduardo around both farms, tending the gardens and animals as well as fixing up the outbuildings and painting some of them. I will pay you the same amount that I pay Eduardo and will take you on a tour of my property later. Oh, by the way, since you look so much like my late husband, except for the beard you are starting to grow, do you mind if I call you by his name, Richard?"

"No, of course not."

Deborah thought that Richard must have amnesia. She told him about amnesia. "Amnesia is a deficit in memory caused by disease, brain damage, or using various hypnotic drugs and sedatives. Due to the extent of damage, memory can be either wholly or partially lost. There are two types of amnesia, anterograde and retrograde. With the first one, people cannot remember things for long periods of time. The second one is what you probably have Richard, which is you do not have the ability to retrieve information that was acquired before your accident. Retrograde amnesia is usually temporary and sometimes can be treated by exposure to the location of events prior to the amnesia. People suffering with amnesia can recall immediate information, and they can form new memories. They can also retain substantial linguistic, intellectual, and social skills despite impairments in the ability to recall specific information before the amnesia. I think we should wait before we seek professional help in Santiago since your previous memories may slowly return. Also, most forms of amnesia fix themselves without being treated.

"By the way, I called two cruise lines that were operating the night of your accident, trying to find out if any passengers were lost at sea, but the managers of the cruise lines told me that they cannot give out that kind of information. Eduardo, Maria, and I assume you must have been in your own boat when it crashed in the wild sea that night, and you managed to swim shore. If anyone was with you, they probably drown."

Richard started to help Deborah and Eduardo tend their gardens, go fishing with them, and take care of repairs on the farmhouse and chicken coop. After about three months, Deborah invited him to go with her to Puerto Williams. There, she introduced him to a few of her friends. Of course, she did not mention Richard's accident and his memory loss but just introduced him as a visiting friend. After their return from Puerto Williams, Deborah told Richard, "I love to travel, but my late husband never wanted to travel much, even around Chile. Since you told me that you seem to like traveling, let us take a trip to Southwest Patagonia. I will arrange the trip with a tour company I have used before, and you can use my late husband's passport since you resemble him so much."

Chapter 2
Travels in South America

I

Richard and Deborah started their Patagonia adventure early on a Saturday morning by catching a flight to Puerto Natales via Punta Arenas. That night, they stayed at the Lighthouse Hotel in separate rooms with wonderful views of the Andes. After dinner at the hotel, the couple had a walk around the nice small town and came across many young folks having a good time. They continued their walk in the town the next morning, but this time they went down to the large Fjord that was fed by the Pacific Ocean with a lighthouse nearby. They both were very hungry, so after their return to the hotel, they had breakfast. After a delicious meal, their driver came and took them to the pier, where a small ship was docked. The tour boat held about twenty-four passengers.

Their boat ride, which took about an hour with cocktails on the way, was to the Ultima Esperanza Fjord for a visit to the Balmaceda and Serrano glaciers, which are in Bernardo O'Higgins National Park. After disembarking, Deborah, Richard, and their fellow passengers took an hour hike around the area that was rough in places, and they even had to walk across two swinging bridges. At the end of the walk, everyone enjoyed the great views of Grey Glacier, a great ice mass, and the surrounding mountains.

At lunch, the group watched a hungry fox circling nearby and listened to their guide, Ruth, giving an excellent talk about the glaciers and why they are receding in Chile. She said after Antarctica and the high Arctic, Chile has the third largest number of glaciers. Ruth went on to say that she thought the receding of their glaciers is from less cold and snow, not climate change. She explained that glaciers are formed from falling snow and that it must be cold and snowy for a long time for ice to accumulate and become part of a glacier.

In the afternoon, the group was transferred to the area of Grey Lake to start a boat ride across the lake that was part of Grey Glacier. The boat ride gave Richard, Deborah, two Spaniards, two Brazilians, and four Russians a chance of staying at the front of the main wall of Grey Glacier, a magnificent natural marvel that is an important part of the Southern Ice Field. Later, they saw more glaciers and then went to Torres del Paine National Park by van, where the members of the small group went to different hotels. Richard and Deborah were taken to the Tyndall Hotel, and it reminded him of the movie *The Shining*, starring Jack Nicholson. He was surprised that he remembered the movie. They were the only ones at the hotel besides a weird old lady cook and Jose, a strange-appearing waiter, who was also the front desk clerk. The couple enjoyed the food—soup, bread, and pasta. Jose had studied at the University in Florida and had been in other U.S. states, and the more he talked, the more worried Richard got, feeling that Jose hated people and seemed a little crazy. Later, the couple went to their separate rooms. Richard had a restless night thinking of Jose coming into his room with a big knife.

After their breakfast in the hotel, they joined their group and went into Torres del Paine National Park by van to see more glaciers in the distance. They stopped at one overlook to admire the unmatched panoramic view of the area and later visited Nordenskjold Lake, Salto Grande, and Pehoe. After finishing the park tour, they returned to the hotel.

The second night at the hotel was not as frightening for Richard as a couple, Tim and Sarah, checked in and joined them at dinner. Sarah was a professor in Austin, Texas, and they were headed for Bakersfield, California, where Tim planned to teach. Deborah and Richard listened to Sarah describe her undergraduate studies at the University of Colorado; following her good time in Boulder, she went to Berkeley, where she received her PhD and met Tim. Something about what Sarah had said brought back some memories of the University of Colorado for Richard.

On Monday morning, the couple and other visitors left the national park by bus and had a long drive, about 140 miles, to Punta Arenas. On the ride, Richard saw that the driver was waving at cars/buses/trucks going by, especially in leaving the national park, something he remembered about Southern folks in the United States. The country was very flat with lots of horses, cattle, and sheep grazing on the grass land. The bus passed many farms and went through several small towns. At one point, the bus stopped at a border check point, where there was another road that led to nearby Argentina.

Richard and Deborah spent the night in separate rooms at a Punta Arenas hotel near the sea. The next morning, they had a walk down to the port and admired a monument on the parkway. After a late breakfast, a driver came and took them to the nice and modern airport with excellent security. They left Punta Arena in the early afternoon for home.

On the flight, Deborah had the aisle seat, Richard had the middle one, and an elderly lady had the window seat. After takeoff, Deborah fell asleep. Richard noticed that the elderly lady was carrying a small medical bag and asked if she was a doctor. She knew some English and said she was a healer. She told him that her name was Ligia Castillo and lived in Puerto Williams. Richard said he had problems with his memory. She then asked him if she could do some therapy on him. He agreed, and the first thing she told Richard was to press his thumb very hard under his nose while exhaling and do this three times. She also held Richard's hands and kept stroking his middle finger on his right hand to release his built-up stress and trouble. She did this ten times and then threw the stress from her hand downward. Richard felt much better and thought that he remembered something of his childhood. Then she read Richard's hand and told him that the line perpendicular to his middle finger shows strong intelligence and that the line running from his middle finger down his palm to his wrist shows his lifeline; the middle of the line was broad and deeper, and she said it indicated a bad or hard time in his life. She then put her hand over his forehead and said she was sending him universal love. About that time, the plane started descending into Puerto Williams, and that woke Deborah.

II

About a month after their first trip, Deborah invited Richard to go on a prearranged trip to the northern part of Chile. A week later, they board a flight to Santiago via Punta Arenas. They spent the night at the Sheraton Hotel in Santiago in separate rooms. The next morning, they took a two-hour flight to Calama, a city near the Peruvian and Bolivian border that was once part of Bolivia. The terrain between Santiago and Calama is very mountainous, and near Calama, it looks like Death Valley in the United States, flat land with lots of sand. Upon arrival in Calama, there were strong winds, resulting in a dust storm. Their tour driver/guide, Rodrigo, was waiting for the couple and said that the weather did not make it safe enough for their drive to San Pedro de Atacama. So he took them to the nearby five-star Park Plaza Hotel. There were few guests at the hotel, and the front desk clerk told them that during the weekend, most of the two hundred rooms are filled. After a first-class buffet lunch, the couple went to their rooms for a nap and, later, dinner. At the time, a couple from Amsterdam had just ridden their bikes from the airport. They had on raincoats and were very wet and windblown. It had even started to snow.

Following breakfast the next morning, Richard and Deborah waited for their ride to the village of San Pedro de Atacama. The front desk clerk told them that the last snowstorm was in 1993. Later, Deborah got a call from Rodrigo that the road had opened between the two cities and that he would be there right after an early lunch. On the way to San Pedro, which was about an hour drive on a nice two-lane paved highway, there were many cars stopped along the way with families having snowball fights and making snowmen. Most of the snowmen were placed on the hoods of the cars. Thus, as they drove along the highway, many cars were going to Calama with snowmen on their car hoods. It looked very funny, of course. Rodrigo did most of the talking on the drive, telling the couple about the area and what they would see. He said that he had a wife and two young children and had been taking people on tours since high school.

Later on the drive, the flat terrain changed from snow-covered to brown land with a few small hills. As they approached San Pedro, there were high mountains and volcanoes. One volcano was even emitting smoke. As the threesome were coming into the city, they went by a series of big slanted red rocks that the locals called dinosaur ridge. The beautiful rocks looked like the backs of giant lizards.

San Pedro is a small town of approximately 3,500 inhabitants and has an elevation of 7,200 feet. Rodrigo dropped the couple in front of the Kimal hotel. The street was muddy as were most of the other streets in the town. They both tracked mud into the small reception area and later into their room that they had to share. The hotel was rated four stars, but it was more like an American motel of one or two stars. The room was small with twin beds, no television, and only a small shower. There was a sign near the toilet that read, "No paper down the toilet," in both English and Spanish. Deborah apologized to Richard that when she made the reservations for the trip, this was the only hotel in town with a vacancy.

Later that afternoon, Rodrigo took the couple out to the Atacama Salt Flat. It was about a thirty-minute ride from town, and they passed a radio observatory rated as the most powerful one in the world; Rodrigo said that there are scientists from many countries doing research at the observatory. They also passed through the village of Tacoma. Lake Chata is situated on the expansive Salt Flats of the Flamingos National Reserve, and the threesome had a nice walk on a salt path around one of the lakes full of three different species of beautiful flamingos. In the distance were several volcanoes of the Andes mountain chain. On the way back to San Pedro, they had a brief stop in Tacoma, renowned for its classic bell tower. Back in San Pedro, Richard had a short walk around the village on the muddy streets and saw many dogs and two black cats. He was told later by Rodrigo that most of the dogs are strays and do not have owners.

After dinner in a nearby small restaurant, the couple returned to their room. They had a long discussion of the wonderful things they had seen during the day. The discussion ended by Richard saying, "Thank you, Deb, for arranging such a fantastic trip, just like the one to Patagonia, and for taking such good care of me at the farm."

"Thank you as well for coming into my life and making it like a wonderful dream."

Then she gave him a loving hug and said good night.

Early the next morning, the couple was picked up and taken to see the Geysers del Tatio. Rodrigo had warned Richard and Deborah that it would be very cold at the geysers. The couple had only light jackets with them, so they both wore their pajamas under their pants and short sleeve shirts and put on two pairs of socks. The drive was over a washboard, narrow and muddy road. The fast and scary drive in the dark took about an hour. The enduring ride was worth it to see many steaming geysers, several of which were erupting boiling water several feet in the air. The fourteen-thousand-foot elevated area was mostly surrounded by volcanoes, and there were some old stone dwellings used by travelers in the past. Before they left the area, all three had a picnic breakfast in the car.

The ride back to San Pedro was slower, so the couple could

admire the beautiful valley along the way. They passed a few more small rock dwellings, green fields, and a stream and saw several llamas. They also had excellent views of the Torcopuri and Sairecabur volcanoes.

In the afternoon, the group had a scenic drive to Salt Mountain and Valle de Marte (Chile's Death Valley) and had a long walk up one of the picturesque canyons. In the evening, they watched a spectacular sunset in the extraordinary landscape of Moon Valley, which has one of the largest salt flats in the world.

Late the next morning, Richard and Deborah were on their way back to Santiago. After their arrival at the Sheraton, Richard told Deborah, "I think I am starting to remember some things in the past. Although I did not remember being in Santiago when we stayed here several days ago, now I think I have been in the city before, maybe several years ago. I think I attended a conference in this hotel, and I recognize some of the buildings in the city."

Deborah replied with a smile on her face, "That is great, Richard! Maybe where we go in the next few days will also help you remember more of your former life. I have arranged a ride for us to go to Viña del Mar and Valparaíso, next to the ocean. First, though, I want to show you around Santiago and the area where I grew up."

Following the visits, they went for a walk over to the newer part of Santiago, where the tallest building in South America is being built. In the area, there were plenty of folks on the sidewalks and in the many stores.

In the late afternoon, they went by bus down to the Pacific Ocean to visit Viña del Mar and Valparaíso. These coastal cities are about a ninety-minute drive from Santiago. The trip took the couple through the central valley, famous for its wines, fruits, and cheese. Viña del Mar was initially a land of wineries, but today it is Chile's most important beachside city. After arrival, they checked into the Sheraton Miramar, a plush five-star hotel. They made an early night of it since they were going to have a long walk around Viña del Mar after an early breakfast.

The next day, they spent all morning touring the old part of the city. "It was very interesting," commented Richard over lunch at McDonald's.

"Yes, I do love this city, mainly because of its location next to the beautiful ocean."

After a Big Mac lunch, they noticed a lot of big stray dogs, some sleeping and others walking around. The dogs seemed to know when to cross the street with the green light. Some of them needed a veterinarian; one dog had a back leg that she could not walk on. They also saw a man picking through the trash can and eating what food he found as he continued his search for more discarded food. Later, the guy found a gold mine of food in another trash can and took a seat outside to consume his find. Deborah had not eaten all her french fries, so Richard put some money on her tray with the fries, and as they were leaving for another walk, he placed her tray on the poor soul's table. Deborah told Richard that he was kind and generous.

In the early afternoon, the couple took a taxi to the adjoining town, Valparaíso, for $20. Valparaíso was declared by the UNESCO as a World Heritage Site in 2003. Its buildings have unique architecture and were built on forty-one hills. It also has one of Chile's main ports. Richard and Deborah went for a long walk around the city and found out that except for a couple of long streets near the port, the other streets are narrow and steep. Richard told Deborah that it is a nice old town but thought Viña del Mar is better. They had an early dinner at a pizza restaurant. After dinner, there was rush-hour traffic, and they had trouble finding a return taxi. After stopping several taxis, the drivers told them that they were not going in the direction of Viña del Mar. The couple finally got a taxi that was going in their direction. There were already two other passengers in the taxi. Then the cabbie picked up another passenger, but despite the crowded condition in the car, they got back to their hotel for less than $2.

The next morning, after returning to the Sheraton in Santiago by bus, the couple took a bus tour of the city. They heard many interesting facts about the city. The guide's narrative started with a reminder that Santiago is ringed by the Andes Mountains and was shaped by the contributions of Chile's indigenous population and a dozen different European cultures.

"Its history dates to 1541, when it was founded by the Spanish conquistador Pedro de Valdivia. Towards the end of the nineteenth century, Santiago became a national territory supported by the wealth generated from nitrate mining. A major urban remodeling was undertaken, which was greatly influenced by French and Italian neoclassical architecture. By the beginning of the twentieth century, Santiago's population was in the range of three hundred thousand inhabitants. However, during the 1950s and 1960s, the city's population jumped above two million, and the urbanization expanded in all directions. Now Santiago has a population of approximately six and a half million, which represents around 40 percent of Chile's population."

On the tour, the passengers visited the Plaza de Armas square that exists because when the Spaniards established cities, they always used a central point as the axis of their city plans. From the Plaza de Armas stop, the group visited some of the city's most relevant historic buildings, which included the Metropolitan Cathedral, Santiago City Hall, Central Post Office, Casa Colorada and Santiago Museum, National Congress, Royal House of Customs and Pre-Colombian museum, Judicial Palace, and Palacio de la Real Audiencia and National Historic Museum.

After lunch, the tour continued in a van by going to Concha y Toro Winery with seven others, plus a guide and a driver. The winery is in the picturesque rural setting of Pirque, only an hour drive out of Santiago. At the winery, the group learned about the growth and development of the vines and visited its ancient cellars, which included the "Casillero del Diablo" (Devil's Cellar), where they heard the legend that has made Chilean wine known worldwide. The group also got to see the owner's historic summerhouse. At the end of the tour, everyone was offered red wine to taste. All the guests, including Deborah and the guide, took a glass except Richard. After everyone had finished toasting and drinking of the wine, the guide asked Richard why he did not take his glass of wine. Richard replied that he did not drink. So the guide quickly took Richard's glass and gulped the wine down in two seconds.

Following the winery visit, the group went up to the Valle Nevado ski area in the Andes. The ride up in the small van was scary for the couple and the other passengers. The driver drove too fast, and one person got sick. The trip to the ski area was about thirty miles long with sixty-one hairpin curves. The Nevado ski area is nine thousand feet high with wonderful views of the surrounding mountains. The weather was great with blue skies, and everyone only wore light jackets despite snow on the ground. The ride back to Santiago was a little calmer than the ride up.

The next morning, Deborah told Richard that she had invited an old friend to have breakfast with them. "Coni and I went through medical school together. She has worked at the main hospital in Santiago since her internship and has a husband and two grown children. I have already told her a lot about you."

"That sounds fine. I hope you only told her the good things about me."

"Yes, indeed, you funny clown."

The threesome met in the hotel lobby, and after introductions, they went to the hotel restaurant. The two ladies did most of the talking during the meal, catching up on their activities since they were last together two years ago. Following the meal, Coni went to work, and the couple took a long walk behind the hotel up Cerro San Cristobal Mountain that has spectacular views of the city. They also saw the white statue of Jesus, a beautiful church, and the zoo from the viewpoint. They then went to explore the old city center. They spent some time in the church square, where plenty of artists were painting, singers singing, and bands playing. The morning ended in a big church where an orchestra was playing wonderful music, and they sat there for a while enjoying the music, along with many others.

After lunch in the city and a cab ride to the airport, they flew back to Puerto Williams. Fall weather also arrived as the couple had to start wearing heavy coats. Richard continued his work around the farm as well as helping Eduardo with his chores. Deborah started playing and singing lots of new music in the evenings following delightful dinners. She and James's loving friendship continued to grow.

One cold day Deborah told Richard that she was ready to experience some warmer weather. She asked him if he would like to go with her for several weeks of touring a few other countries in South America. Of course, he agreed. So she started organizing the trips and making reservations.

III

The happy couple flew to Rio de Janeiro via Punta Arenas, Puerto Natales, and Santiago and stayed at a five-star hotel in the Copacabana area. After checking in and leaving their luggage in their separate rooms, they took a five-block walk to the beautiful Copacabana Beach. The waves were remarkably high, and there were a few surfers on the waters, a couple of hang gliders in the sky, and lots of sunbathers on the beach. It had rained during their taxi ride to the hotel, but now it was sunny and warm. There were lots of street vendors on the beach selling hats, sunglasses, water, T-shirts, and a variety of other items. The couple continued their walk following a late lunch at Burger King. Along one stretch of the street near the hotel were about a dozen homeless young men sleeping on the sidewalk on old mattresses, covered with blankets.

The next morning after breakfast, Richard and Deborah started an all-day city tour in a minibus, along with ten other tourists. The group visited Corcovado mountain, where Christ the Redeemer statue is located. One can see the Atlantic Ocean and most of Rio from the bottom of the statue.

After a buffet lunch, the group took two exciting cable car rides to Sugarloaf Mountain. There, they had a wonderful view of Rio, the Copacabana, Ipanema, and Leblon. The trip ended with a city tour passing by the downtown area, Maracana, San Sebastian Cathedral, and Sambodomo. Their tour guide dropped the couple off at the beach near their hotel, where they enjoyed watching a half a dozen young boys playing soccer on the beach. It seemed like every player was trying to win as they did not form teams. It was like cutthroat pool. Richard exchanged $100 for 300 reais at a local exchange store before they headed back to the hotel.

On their last full day in Rio, both Richard and Deborah slept in and then went down for a late breakfast. The rest of the morning was spent doing some shopping in nearby stores. In the afternoon and evening, they took a couple of long walks, one near the hotel and the other along the beach. They stayed at the beach until it got dark. There were plenty of people walking on the sidewalk paralleling the beach and lots of vendors displaying their goods for sale. Sugarloaf Mountain was visible from the beach area and a fortress in the opposite direction. Richard told Deborah, "I think Rio is one of the most beautiful and unusual cities we have visited so far, mainly because there are beautiful beaches on one side of the city and fantastic mountains on the three other sides."

"I agree with you, Richard, and the architecture of the buildings are also to be admired. Shall we return to our room now for our last night in the great hotel?"

"Okay, Deb, but are you sure you want to skip dinner?"

"You can go ahead and eat, but the late breakfast where I pigged out is enough for me. Say, I have an idea, instead of going back home, let us see some more of Brazil. I can look into flights out of Rio while you are having dinner."

"I forgot to tell you, Deb, that last night I went to the business center in the hotel, where I Goggled the Traveler's Century Club, the organization your friend Coni belongs to. Remember she told us about the club and that she has silver status because of visiting more than 150 countries and territories on the club list of 327. I printed out the club's list of countries and territories that they suggest for visits. The club rules state that one must only step on the ground at an airport to check that country or territory off the list. So in case we join the club someday, we should travel to some of the places on the list. The information is in my room. Please take a look at it. Maybe there are some destinations that they recommend in Brazil. Here is my key card. See you later."

They left the hotel Saturday morning and had a race car driver as a taxi driver. He drove over the speed limit, passing everything on the highway. Most traffic was going into the city. It only took twenty minutes to get to the airport. However, the ride gave them a good view of the large city with its sprawling suburbs. They checked in for their two-hour TAM flight to Salvador that Deborah had arranged the night before.

The plane landed in Salvador, a city of two and a half million in the state of Bahia. Bahia, a religious destination for most visitors, has more than three hundred churches and thousands of candomblé houses of worship that make the state a powerful source of religious faith. Many destinations in Bahia are well-known for their religious attractions, including Salvador, Cachoeira, Santo Amaro, Bom Jesus da Lapa, Canudos, Monte Santo, and Candeias. Salvador has a mixture of individual homes, some nice and others in various stages of construction. There are also many groups of high-rise apartments.

Richard and Deborah stayed at the Cocoo Hotel, and their rooms were like cocoons. The rooms had painted concrete floors and were more like a lower-class Motel 6 in the States with twenty-seven rooms on two floors. The hotel did have a small swimming pool, restaurant, and bar. Following getting settled in their rooms, the couple took a walk down to the beach, about two blocks away on the other side of a six-lane major road that paralleled the beach. The waves were high, and numerous surfers were out on the water. There were few people along the beach, and the area was far from town but only a fifteen-minute taxi ride from the airport. There is another motel nearby called the Hotel Jaguaribe Praia. The area around the hotels is called Praia, and the first thing Richard thought of was a jaguar near a cocoon. A small shopping mall is attached to the Jaguaribe hotel, but most of its shops were vacant. There is also a gas station nearby that has a small convenience store, where the couple bought a few supplies, including water.

It was raining the next morning. Camilla, the beautiful young lady at the front desk, loaned the couple an umbrella that was indeed needed. Richard and Deborah boarded a Salvador tour bus that had arrived near their hotel. There were already about ten passengers who boarded at other hotels between theirs and the airport. The bus driver made three more hotel pickups and then proceeded into the city. On the double-decker bus, the couple soon found out how big the city is. Some of the places the bus went by before an hour break at noon were the Barra Lighthouse, Castro Alves Theatre, Forte de Sao Pedro, and Campo Grande. In the historic center were more than a thousand houses, churches, and monuments built since the sixteenth century, making Salvador the greatest collection of Baroque architectural heritage in Latin American.

The hour's midday break was spent at the Mercado Modelo, a big old structure housing many souvenir shops. Deborah bought a hat and a couple of postcards. Nearby was a marina that had a naval station on the shore, and next door was a beautiful church in need of repairs.

On the way back to the hotel, the driver took the group through the rest of the historic city and into old town. The group had a thirty-minute break at Senhor do Bomfim Church that sits on Mont Serrat, a high point in the city that provides a spectacular panoramic view. The final stop was at the Memorial of Irmã Dulce, which consists of a small church and museum. As a child, Irmã Dulce or "Sweet Sister" used to pray to Santo Antonio, asking for a sign since she wanted to know whether she should follow the path of a religious life. At the age of thirteen, she began to help the poor, the sick, and the helpless. In 1933, she joined the Congregation of Missionary Sisters of the Immaculate Conception of the Mother of God, in our Lady of Carmel Convent, in the State of Sergipe. Upon her return to Bahia, she devoted the remainder of her life to helping the less fortunate. She died in Salvador in 1992 at the age of seventy-seven.

The next morning, the couple left for Recife, the most eastern city in South America. The ride was on an Azul Airlines Embraer 190 plane. About halfway to Recife, the landscape started to get flat and barren.

After arrival in Recife and a taxi ride to the Boa Viagem Praia Hotel, Richard and Deborah got settled into their room that had a partial view of the ocean across a major four-lane road. The twin-bed room was small and not too nice. Later, they had a walk about, and it seemed like there were a lot of cars that were Chevrolets.

The next morning, the couple went back to the airport and caught their Azul flight to Fernando de Noronha Island at nine. About halfway, they had an hour stopover in Natal, a large city with a broad river running through it to the ocean. Almost all the passengers got off except Richard, Deborah, and ten others who continued on the flight to the island.

The plane arrived at Fernando de Noronha with an extremely hard landing as the short runway that was used for landings, takeoffs, and taxiing was in bad shape. The weather was very pleasant. There are several resorts on the island as well as three old fortresses and two churches. The main feature the couple saw from the small one-gate terminal was the extinct Morro do Pico volcano and the smaller Morro do Frances volcano. Richard and Deborah did not leave the airport, and after an hour layover, they returned to Recife.

On the return flight, Richard told Deborah, "Now we can mark Fernando de Noronha on the Traveler's Century Club list of countries and territories. At least we got to see the island from the air during the plane's landing and takeoff."

"I think we should join the club after our return to my home."

The next morning, the couple took a city tour in a minivan with ten other visitors. Their guide did not speak any English, but Deborah understood most of what he said and translated some of it for Richard. He told the group that Recife has a population of five million, whereas Fortaleza has three million. São Paulo and Rio are in first and second place. The weather was perfect, but the traffic was terrible. The group saw much of the big city and stopped at a couple of museums. One museum had manikin replicas of famous people, including Elvis and the Pope, and the other museum had groups of native manikins. They also stopped at a big cathedral that overlooked the city of many high-rise apartments and office buildings. At noon, the group had a buffet lunch, where there were many varieties of food, from Chinese and Japanese to American and Italian. Richard loaded his big plate with numerous dishes, including four pieces of sushi. There was a line of people waiting to pay and go to a table. Meanwhile, Richard ate the sushi and found out when he reached the cashier that she weighed the plate, and the charge was by weight. Richard had gotten some free sushi that Deborah kidded him about over their meal.

After lunch, the driver took the group on a long drive near the city's edge to visit the Ricardo Brennand Institute, which covered a large area with part of it with a fenced-in antelope herd. The mile-long driveway was lined with beautiful palm trees. The museum was housed in two buildings that looked like castles. Ricardo Brennand inherited a vast fortune from his father and collected everything from paintings and sculptures to guns, jewelry, and clocks from around the world. All these things were displayed in a very museum-style manner. There was even a small collection of old-world globes that Richard particularly enjoyed. Outside the buildings were a fountain and some statues of lions.

The next morning, they traveled by taxi to the Recife airport, which is nice with twenty-one gates and even three rooms with beds, where a person can sleep for a price. The couple took a TAM flight to Fortaleza that was about an hour. After arrival at the good-sized Fortaleza airport, they took a thirty-minute taxi ride to the Crocobeach Hotel. The five-star hotel is across a main road from the beach that is lined with many restaurants with outdoor tables. The ocean waves were extremely high, and many surfers were being challenged to stay on their boards.

That afternoon, Richard and Deborah had a short walk along the beautiful beach and then got a taxi ride to the nearby Rio Mar indoor shopping center. Rio Mar has five stories in a large building, where there are two major grocery stores and many shops selling everything from furniture to clothing. There were also many restaurants, including Outback, McDonald's, Burger King, and Subway. The couple had a pizza dinner at Pizza Hut.

The next morning, after a nice buffet breakfast, the couple joined a group of ten for a four-hour city tour. The city is very dense with many high-rise apartments and business buildings, just like in Salvador and Recife. The tour bus went to an old dock area where two large wooden piers, built by the English many years ago, are located. Nearby was one of the oldest houses in Fortaleza. The guide told the group that it was built by a wealthy businessman who had seven sons. After each son grew up and got married, the father had homes constructed near his home as gifts to his sons. During World War II, there was a small American base near the new dock area. The final stop that morning was at an old large open-air structure of six stories housing at least a hundred vendors in their stalls selling everything that anyone would want as well as a restaurant, where the group had lunch. The old building was across the street from a fortress, next to a beautiful and big cathedral.

The next morning, the couple went by taxi to the airport to

catch their TAM airline flight to Rio. The flight took three hours, and they almost missed their flight to Brasilia. When Richard got his boarding pass, the TAM agent told him that he had a corridor seat, not an aisle seat; he thought it was interesting language to use. Following their arrival in Brasilia and checking into the Mercure hotel, they both took a short nap in their separate rooms. After their rest, they had a long walk near the hotel as well as around the shopping mall across from the hotel. There was an excellent food court in the three-story shopping center, which included a Burger King, McDonald's, and Subway. For dinner, they both had a healthy salad at Subway.

The city is very new and planned out with lots of high-rise hotels and office and apartment buildings going up in various areas of the city. There is not a downtown but groups of buildings with shopping malls about ten miles apart connected by four-lane highways with roundabouts at various intersections. It appeared like the bus service was good, with lots of walking paths with underpasses.

The second day, the couple took a city tour. The ten-person tour group went in a minibus. On the tour, the group stayed at eight places for around fifteen minutes each. The first stop was at a new church. Another stop was to see several government buildings. There were also some government buildings at another stop, where there was the changing of the guards. After several more stops, the last one was at the President's Castle that had a fence around it about half a block from the building. There were guards at each corner of the fence and with three flags in the middle outside the fence. Their guide told the group that when all the flags are up, it means that the queen is at home. Of course, the king was at work in the nearby government offices.

As the couple left the hotel on their last morning in Brasilia, there was a lot of traffic that thinned out as they got closer to the airport. Near the airport, there were some areas with single family homes and fewer high-rise buildings. The airport was nice and new with the domestic and international airports next to each other. At the airport, they arranged a direct flight from Manaus to Lima instead of the long flight via São Paulo. The flight from Brasilia to Manaus was about three hours; Manaus is an hour behind Brasilia. Richard was trying to get some sleep on the plane because he did not sleep very well during the previous night as there were some folks in the hallway making lots of noise. He had even called the front desk and complained. To make matters worse, early this morning, one of the hotel neighbors kept saying his prayers very loud and repeating Jesus's name. This was about five. The noise did not bother Deborah, so on the flight, she read about Brazil in the airline magazine. In Manaus, they stayed at the Sleep Inn for two nights.

After getting settled in her room, Deborah booked a tour for the next morning, leaving at nine. That night, they explored a little of the city and a small shopping center near the hotel, where they had dinner. The next morning, they were picked up by taxi and taken to the tour meeting place. There were twenty in the tour group, and after boarding a double-decker boat, they crossed an area where the white Amazon and brown Negro rivers meet. The guide described the area in both English and Spanish. One thing he spoke about was the 200 different kinds of fish in the Amazon, including several different varieties of piranhas. Later, the boat docked at a small village, where the group was divided into several smaller groups for short canoe trips into the backwaters of one of their rivers. The river was surrounded by lots of trees and other vegetation. On the canoe trip, the couple's group saw a small alligator and lots of birds. During the dry months, these small rivers dry up, and boats cannot travel on them. Following the canoe ride, the group returned to the boat and went back to town. The next day, the couple flew to Lima.

IV

The couple arrived in Lima late in the afternoon. Richard was surprised that the Lima airport is big, modern, and busy. After collecting their luggage, they took a taxi in heavy traffic to the Gran Hotel Bolivar. The hotel is in front of the Plaza San Martin. There is a statue of General San Martin in the middle of the plaza that is a block square and surrounded by several beautiful white buildings. One of the buildings is a hospital that used to be a railroad station. Next to the square is a Pizza Hut, and to the left of the hotel is a pedestrian walkway. There is a KFC next to the hotel entrance. During their stay, the couple ate at both places, including the hotel restaurant.

The Gran Hotel Bolivar, the first major modern hotel to be built in Lima, was constructed by an American company, Fred Tiley. Its area is four thousand square yards and was finished on December 9, 1924. There is a 1920 Model T Ford in the lobby. Famous guests were William Faulkner, Ernest Hemingway, Ava Gardner, President Nixon's wife, Clark Gable, Yul Brynner, and Mick Jagger.

Following breakfast the first morning, Richard and Deborah took a long walk in the inner city. It was light-jacket weather. Lima does not get much rain, but the sky was overcast. In the afternoon, Deborah arranged a tour. A taxi picked up the couple at the hotel at two and took them south across town in about thirty minutes in heavy traffic to Miraflores. Deborah took several pictures of the seaside while they waited for the tour van and guide. Two ladies from Ireland joined them as well as their guide. Jason was a nice young man who spoke excellent English. After the van came and the drive started, he told the foursome about the city and country. He said, "There are eleven million people in Lima, and it is divided in forty-three districts. Peru has a population of thirty-two million people. After slavery was abolished, many Chinese came to work here. There is even a Chinatown in Lima. The main industries in the country are mining, fishing, and agriculture."

Following the tour, the couple had a wonderful dinner in the hotel restaurant and discussed the events of the day. Richard thanked her for arranging such a wonderful trip. She said, "I have not been here since I was in college, and I do have more plans for us during the next couple of weeks. The day after tomorrow, we will go to Trujillo then Cusco and Machu Picchu."

After dinner, James walked Deborah to her room and gave her a loving hug with kisses on both cheeks and his sleep well wishes.

Following a late breakfast, the couple took a long walk to the end of the pedestrian street where the cat park is located. Deborah took many pictures of the magnificent old buildings and churches. In the afternoon, they went on another tour with Jason and the van driver. This time their traveling companions were a couple from France who understood Spanish. The trip started in Miraflores again. The van driver first drove around Miraflores and then went south along the coast to a very deserted area, where they toured the Pachacamac Citadel and the Sanctuary of the Pachacamac God, who was considered to be the creator of the universe by the ancient Andean people. The citadel has temples, pyramids, and palaces. The highlights were the Temple of the Sun, the Pachacamac Temple, and the "Acllahuasi" or Palace of the Virgins of the Sun. (Women were sacrificed there.) The group of six had a thirty-minute walk to the top of the Temple of the Sun, the highest point of the area. There, everyone had a great view of several high hills with many homes on them. Next, they visited the historic center of Lima with its palaces, mansions, churches, and squares as well as the monumental compound of San Francisco with its convent and catacombs. There, the group saw at least a hundred skeletons, bones, and skulls. In the main square is a cathedral, bishop's palace, governor's palace, and city hall/parliament. A nearby park is home to over one hundred cats, and a large demonstration was taking place there over low wages.

That evening, after an early dinner at the nearby Pizza Hut, the couple walked from the hotel to the end of the pedestrian mall. The pedestrian walkway was packed with families out enjoying the evening as well as about a dozen street performers. There were three different guys, looking a lot like Michael Jackson, who sang and moved like him. Most impressive was a genie suspended in space over a teapot with no props. Lots of vendors were walking around with trays of goods, mainly snacks, and some of the lady vendors had their small children on their backs. Every shop was closed except casinos, pharmacies, a few small restaurants, KFC, and McDonald's. There were also lots of police near the government buildings at the end of the walkway. After the walk, the couple returned to their rooms to pack and retire for the night.

V

After a late breakfast, James and Deborah checked out at noon and took a taxi to the airport in much traffic. The airport is on the northern end of Lima and next to the ocean. The thirty-minute ride to the airport showed Richard again what a large city Lima is. Unfortunately, their scheduled flight to Trujillo was canceled, so they had a long wait until six in the busy airport for the next flight. The Avianca Peru plane landed in Trujillo a little past seven. The couple then took a twenty-minute ride in the hotel van to the very classy Casa Andina Premium hotel near the center of Trujillo.

Following breakfast the next morning, the couple started walking around the central part of Trujillo. On the walk, they passed a fellow who turned around and said, "John Czermak?"

The couple stopped and turned around. Richard said, "Excuse me?"

"Don't you remember me, John? I am Durado. We went through graduate school together at the University of Colorado. Prof. Harold Dalton was our PhD advisor."

"Now I vaguely remember you, and you might not have recognized me several weeks ago when I had a beard. Please excuse me, but I had a bad accident and lost my memory. Please tell me more about my life. But first let me introduce you to Dr. Deborah Klose. She is a medical doctor and saved my life at Cape Horn in Chile. Can we go somewhere and discuss this more?"

The threesome went to a nearby café and ordered coffee. Over coffee, Durado started his recollection of his friendship with John. "As I mentioned earlier, both of us went through graduate school at the University of Colorado and did our PhD research in the same laboratory. You made three visits here, the first one following a conference in Santiago, the second time when you and Margrit came before your trip to Cusco and Machu Picchu, and the third time three years ago, again following a conference in Santiago."

"Who is Margrit?" a surprised Czermak asked.

Durado laughed. "She is your wife whom you married while in graduate school, and you have three children. At the time, you were working at Rocky Flats full time and attending graduate school full time. After graduating, you became manager of plutonium chemistry research and development at Rocky Flats. A few years later, you had some hard times when you lost your security clearance. Then you went to Australia to teach for three years, followed by returning to a DOE facility in California. Your last visit here was when you worked in California. Amy, your eldest daughter, and Eric are married, and Lorrie is studying at the University of Colorado."

"I am very shocked that I have a wife and three children. But now I am starting to remember a few things. On my last visit here, you and your driver took me to your tanning factory and out of the city to see the ruins of an old fortress. I also remember accidentally running into friends years ago, just like I ran into you today. The first time was accidentally meeting a Russian friend in a Toronto restaurant following a trip to the high arctic. The other time was when I was waiting at a train station in a small German village. I looked across the tracks, and there was a former student of mine from Australia. We exchanged greetings before one of the trains arrived."

Deborah spoke up and said, "Richard, I mean John, has retrograde amnesia that was probably caused by accidental brain damage after being washed up on shore during the night of a violent storm off Cape Horn. We assumed he was in his yacht that sank. He did not have the ability to retrieve information that was acquired before his accident. Retrograde amnesia is usually temporary and sometimes can be treated by exposure to the location of events prior to the amnesia. People suffering with amnesia can recall immediate information, and they can form new memories. They can also retain substantial linguistic, intellectual, and social skills despite impairments in the ability to recall specific information before the amnesia. Also, most forms of amnesia fix themselves without being treated.

"A week after John's accident, I told him that we should wait before we seek professional help in Santiago since his previous memories may slowly return. I live in a remote location on Navarino Island near Port Williams, the most southerly city in the world. My few friends call me a hermit as I have little contact with the outside world since my husband died almost two years ago. Thus, I had no knowledge of John's accident from the news. John did start remembering a few things about Santiago while we were there last week, and I am sure now that he will start remembering more about his previous life and hopefully will get memory back with your help but perhaps not the very unpleasant events of his past."

John told Durado, "Now I vaguely remember that I am a professor at Clemson University in South Carolina, and there, I used my middle name, James, instead of John. I was on an expedition in Antarctica with two of my graduate students and a postdoc from China whom I married on ship. I do not remember if Margrit died or we divorced. On the way back from the expedition, my graduate student from Russia and I accidentally fell overboard near Cape Horn during a violent storm. Since my student could not swim, I tried to rescue him, but he disappeared in the raging waters. By then, the ship was too far away to swim to, but I could vaguely see that land was closer. It was extremely hard to swim through the large waves. About halfway to shore, I was about to give up, but God suddenly appeared and told me I must continue to swim ashore and not die because I still have too much to contribute to the world. The next thing I remember is Deborah attending to me the next morning on the rocky beach."

Following more discussions of Cermak's life, the threesome ordered lunch. After a light meal, Durado said, "If you agree, let me call my driver, and he can take us for a drive around the city, followed by seeing the ruins of the old fortress. Then we can return to the main square where we met this morning. John—or should I start calling you John James?—we can then show Deborah the beautiful cathedral and several old buildings surrounding the park. As you may remember, James, nearby is an old church that was converted into a small university building where I received my undergraduate degree in chemical engineering. This is also where Professor Dalton taught on his sabbatical. This building is now part of the university campus, where several new buildings were built."

Following the visit to the fortress and a long walk around the city center, Durado told the couple that he must return to work. They agreed to meet the next day at the hotel so Durado could show them his farm and home as well as his bottling company. James thanked him with a hug for bringing some of his memory back. He told Deborah that he was very tired and would return to the hotel, skip dinner, and make an early night of it. He asked her to see more of the city and do some shopping if she wished.

After a late breakfast the next day, Durado and his driver picked the couple up and went to his bottling plant for a tour. The plant produces bottled water and a soft drink. Next, they went out of the city to his farm. The farm has a small house, where a couple of workers stay, several farm buildings, and a big swimming pool in the backyard. The main business on the property is raising guineas pigs for several meat markets and growing asparagus for canning. Following the tour of the large farm, the lady of the house prepared a nice lunch for them. James thought the meat was chicken, but Durado told him after the meal that the meat was guinea pig, not chicken. James replied that it was an excellent meal. The final stop in the afternoon was at Durado's home in the city. He had inherited the fifty-year-old house from his parents. The most impressive room in the home was Durado's office with library. He must have had over a hundred books, including a couple that James had written.

The three sat at a large table, and while drinking tea, Durado and James started talking about their time at the University of Colorado. Durado said, "James, do you remember the time when you were distilling some extremely smelly liquid in the lab, and it overheated and sprayed all over the lab bench? Everyone on our floor had to evacuate because of the horrible odor of the chemical."

"Yes, I remember that well since I thought my research days were over. But I cleaned up the mess, and you and the other students returned to their laboratories. The other thing that stands out in my mind is going to an American Chemical Society meeting in Mexico City. Professor Dalton and his wife were with us as well as Margrit. We had been warned by Dalton not to drink the water. However, at the opening ceremony, they were serving margaritas. Mine was warm, so without thinking, I went over to where they were serving drinks and asked the bartender to chip off some ice from a big block of ice and put it in my drink. After drinking the margarita, I realized the ice was probably made from tap water. Sure enough, I was sick all night and did not get any sleep." Everyone laughed.

"Well, Durado, I think we need to go back to the hotel and get ready for our return to Santiago via Lima tomorrow morning. I can't tell you how great it was to see you and for bringing most of my memory back."

Deborah also thanked Durado as the couple got into the car for their return to the hotel.

Deborah and James left Trujillo early the next morning for Lima. During the flight, Deborah started the conversation. "As you know, I had arranged a trip to Cusco and Machu Picchu, but with you discovering your identity from Durado, I think it is best to cancel the remaining visits so we can go to the American Embassy in Santiago and arrange a passport for your return to South Carolina. I am also sorry I did not do more to help you regain your memory. I guess I wanted you to stay with me forever."

Following their return to Santiago late in the afternoon, they went to the American Embassy. After a long wait, James explained to one of the officials that he lost his memory for almost a year because of an accident, and now it had mostly returned. He told the official that the lady with him was a medical doctor and could vouch for his story. He then got fingerprinted and his picture taken. Since the State Department had a file on James, they gave him a copy, along with a new passport.

After checking into a hotel near the airport, James planned, with Deborah's help, to fly to Atlanta the next morning. After calling the Clemson University and leaving a note for Ying to meet him at the Atlanta airport, he went to the hotel's business center and Googled his name. There, he was surprised to find considerable information about his professional career. He printed out a copy of several entries and took them to the room he was sharing with Deborah. He showed the Google and State Department's information to a surprised Deborah. She was amazed by his professional accomplishments and the awards he had received. He told her that hopefully his return to his family and work could bring back all his memories.

After breakfast the next morning, he sadly told Deborah goodbye and thanked her for all her help with a loving hug and kiss and saying, "I love you dearly, but I hope you understand that I have a wife waiting for me in South Carolina. I will miss you so much."

With tears in her eyes, Deborah managed to say "I also love you and thank you for the work you have done for me as well as bringing so much happiness into my life this past year. Goodbye, my dear, until we meet again."

Chapter 3
Return to South Carolina

I

Upon James's arrival in Atlanta, he did not have any checked luggage to look for since he had been using Richard's clothes during his stay at Deborah's. He did have a small carry-on containing some toiletries. Thus, he went directly to immigration. After the agent checked him into the country and stamped his passport, he asked James to wait a minute. He came back a couple of minutes later with another man. The other official asked James to follow him, and they went to an immigration office. There, the man identified himself as an FBI agent and showed James his credentials. The agent started asking questions about his trip to Antarctica and the last night aboard ship. After James told him of his ordeal and his stay with Deborah, the agent said that their interviews with his wife and student confirmed that the death of his Russian student was accidental. The agent thanked James for his cooperation.

Then James breezed through customs and went to the arrivals hall to be met by an overjoyed and tearful Ying and Shanna. There were a few minutes of a loving embrace of the couple, followed by James receiving a hug from Shanna. The ladies were overjoyed with happiness that James was alive and well and had returned as everyone had assumed he and Alex were both lost at sea.

Following the happy reunion, the threesome went to an airport café to catch up on one another's lives. After going to a quiet area of the café with their coffee, Ying started the conversation. "After our arrival back in South Carolina almost a year ago, very distraught, we tried to resume our lives.

Meanwhile, we continued to make inquiries of the ship's owner and captain. The ship officials all contended that you and Alex fell overboard without life jackets in the terrible storm and certainly drown and were eaten by sharks. After a month back at Clemson, I was appointed lecturer in the chemistry department, and Shanna and a couple of your other students graduated. Shanna plans on continuing with a postdoc position in the chemistry department."

James continued the conversation describing the last year with Deborah and their travels. The threesome then leaves the airport and return to Pendleton in Shanna's car. James's son and two daughters surprise him at his and Ying's home, and they have a wonderful reunion with James, telling everyone about his time in Chile and the kind and generous Deborah. Ying and Shanna prepared a delicious dinner that everyone enjoyed with their lively conversations. The three young adults spend two nights at the Pendleton home before returning to Colorado.

Following the departure of his children, James drives to his department's building at the Research Park to be greeted by fellow faculty members, staff, and students. They have a long reunion with James summarizing his year in South America. The exchange of information continues in the break room for the individuals who did not have to go to their classes. After the lengthy reunion, James goes to his office to catch up on his mail and e-mails.

Later, James finds out that his remaining students have been transferred to the supervision of other professors. Late in the afternoon, the dean of engineering and science calls him and welcomes him back. He tells James that the chairman of the chemistry department had retired and that he would like James to take over the department. James readily accepts to the change in jobs.

The next morning, as James is packing his books and papers to move to the chemistry building, a CNN representative with cameraman and several newspaper reporters come to his office, wanting to get the story of his ordeal. In the following days, most newspapers around the world would print his story, including the Russian newspaper *Pravda*.

II

Following James's return, the couple resumes their leisurely routine. Periodically, they host a dinner party at their home for their students and a few faculty members. Of course, the two students living in their basement are always invited to these dinners. The Czermaks also participate in a dinner rotation party with their nearest neighbors. The young lady next door, who is also a faculty member at Clemson, had adopted a five-year-old Chinese girl; of course, Ying sees the girl every chance she gets. Their other activities in the area are working out at the gym, swimming, and playing golf, tennis, chess, and pool. They also attend plays at the nearby Clemson Playhouse and go to some of the Clemson football games during the season. On weekends, they take short car trips or work in their garden. James also renews his love of photography.

One night at dinner, Ying tells James, "Yesterday I received a letter from my best friend Damay who lives in Hong Kong. She had taken a trip to Vietnam and wrote a story about the adventure. She sent me a copy. It is an interesting write-up. Would you like to read the story tonight?"

"Okay, I have some time now, so let me take a look at it."

On the first day of the trip, I flew from Hong Kong to Hanoi on an Air China flight that arrived at one in the afternoon. In the Hanoi airport arrivals area, I met our Global Exchange tour guide, Thao, who will be with us the whole trip, and the other members of our group: Ben, George, Mark, Elena, and Fumi. Our local guide, Leo, who has a college degree in tourism, was also at the airport. He and the driver took the seven of us to the Lenid Hotel Tho Nhuom.

My room was nice, and I had a wonderful bath in a large tub. That evening, I met some of the group for dinner. Thao is from Huo, Vietnam, and now works in Germany. She is married to a German. George, Ben, and Mark also joined us for dinner. All three are attorneys. George and Mark are from Spokane, and Ben lives in a small town north of Seattle. On the four-block walk to the nice and busy Cuisine Viet restaurant, we crossed the street in the middle of the block, and Ben almost got hit by a motorcyclist. On the way back following dinner, I almost got hit crossing the street with a green light. We were told by Thao that some of the motorbike drivers do not stop for red lights. The area between the hotel and the restaurant is nice, but some cars were blocking the sidewalks, and there are many tripping hazards. A variety of shops are in the area.

Following breakfast at the hotel, there was an orientation meeting about the trip with Leo in a private area of the hotel's lobby. Our first visit was to the Thanh Xuan Peace Village, where we got to see the Temple of Literature and Ethnic Minority Museum. At noon, we got to experience the entertaining chanting of a monk and a vegetarian lunch at the Than Quang pagoda. After lunch, we returned to the center of the city and had an easy walking tour with a historian to visit the famed Old Quarter with its bustling streets, shops, and old-style tube houses. Before returning to the hotel, we visited Hoan Kiem Lake. A block away from the hotel is the Hoa Lo Prison. It used to be the "hell on our earth" prison at the heart of Hanoi during the

French colonization period. Then it was regarded by the Vietnamese patriotic soldiers as a school (1896–1954). Later, it was named as Hilton Hanoi by U.S. pilots who were arrested in the northern part of Vietnam (1964–1973). John McCain was one of their prisoners whose plane was shot down on October 26, 1967. Following the depressing visit to the prison, we had dinner at the Cuisine Viet restaurant.

After breakfast at the hotel the next morning, we checked out and boarded a big bus for a four-hour, one-hundred-mile drive to Ha Long Bay. On the drive down on a four-lane highway, we went through several small cities between lots of rice fields. Most of the homes are narrow, long, and three stories high. We stopped about halfway at a large art store full of various paintings, sculptures, weavings as well as a restaurant with toilets; they call the toilets happy rooms. Another stop was at a large pearl store, where we were shown how pearls are made in oysters. The shop had hundreds of pearl jewelry, from rings to necklaces to earrings. I bought a beautiful necklace for a reasonable price.

Ha Long Bay has thousands of spectacular inlets and grottoes rising from the clear emerald Gulf of Tonkin. The islands in Ha Long Bay are mainly limestone and schist islands, mostly lying in three areas: Ha Long in the southwest, Bai Tu Long in the southeast, and Lan Ha in the south. The area is recognized as a World Natural Heritage site with 775 islands, 250–280 million years old. They are the result of the rising and lowering processes of the continent to form a karst. The process of nearly full erosion and weathering of the karst created the unique bay.

Upon arrival at the bay, we were transported to

the Starlight cruise ship with thirty-two beautiful air-conditioned and roomy cabins with television and queen bed. The ship has three decks plus a top open deck as well as a Jacuzzi, restaurant, library, gift shop, and spa.

Following check-in, a welcome drink, and unloading our luggage, everyone received a lunch of fresh seafood while the ship started its cruse in the bay. In the afternoon, everyone enjoyed the spectacular scenery from the sundeck. After the boat anchored off at a quiet designated spot, we had dinner, followed by going to our cabins for the night.

The next morning, breakfast was served while we continued our cruise around Ha Long Bay, passing by many islets named by their shapes such as Dog, Incense Urn, Fighting Cock, Finger, etc. We had a short stop to explore Surprise Cave, one of the most beautiful places in the bay. The ship then continued cruising toward the wharf. We disembarked at ten and started our four-hour drive to Noi Bai airport in Hanoi.

About twenty miles from Hanoi, we had a stop in Bac Ninh province to visit Dinh Bang village and its communal house. There, we got to enjoy Quan Ho folk songs (duo of love songs) performed by villagers. Quan Ho singing is a Vietnamese folk music style with alternating groups of female and male singers issuing musical challenges and responses in the repertoire deal with topics of love and sentimentality. It was recognized as the intangible cultural heritage by the UNESCO in 2009. After a delicious lunch, we continued the drive to Noi Bai airport in Hanoi, arriving at five, where we said goodbyes to our wonderful local guide and bus driver.

Our Vietnam Airlines flight from Hanoi to Dong

Hoi City, Quang Binh province, was an hour and a half. The city sits next to the north central coast of Vietnam and is known as the "City of Roses." It suffered greatly during the Vietnam War. Upon arrival and meeting our new driver and local guide, who was born in the Czech Republic and came here at age one with his parents, we went to a restaurant in Dong Hoi City for dinner. After a great meal, we were taken by bus to Chay Lap Farmstay in Phong Nha-Ke Bang National Park zone, a twenty-five-mile drive. Following check-in, we had a pleasant overnight stay at the farm.

I took a nice walk around the farm the next morning before breakfast. Over breakfast, the group was told that part of a King Kong movie was filmed at the farm; there is a large ceramic hand in the garden representing King Kong's hand. At eight, we had a six-mile bus drive from the farm to the Phong Nha caves. There, we took a thirty-minute motorboat tour inside the Wet Cave. Following the boat ride, we walked up on about a hundred small steps from the mouth of the Wet Cave to the Dry Cave. The group explored the cave for about thirty minutes. At the mouth of the cave, we had a great view of the nearby beautiful mountains and hills covered in trees and shrubs—a real jungle. Following the difficult walk, we returned to the boat for a ride across the river to have lunch at the Oxalis Café.

After a buffet lunch, we had a short bus ride to the Phong Nha-Ke Bang National Park. There, we took a one-hour walk through the Phong Nha Botanical Garden to visit the spectacular Gio Waterfall at Vang Anh Lake. Next, we took a bus ride over part of the historic Ho Chi Minh Trail and had a stop to visit Eight Ladies Cave. At this cave on

November 14, 1972, bombs from American planes were dropped, collapsing the entrance and trapping eight volunteer youth inside. Rescue efforts failed, and all perished. At four, we returned to Chay Lap Farmstay to relax before dinner at seven.

After breakfast the next morning we checked out of the farm and started our 120-mile bus ride to Hue. After about a two-and-a-half-hour drive, we stopped for a visit at Vinh Moc tunnels; the tunnels were built to shelter people from the intense bombing during the war. Next, we had an hour journey to Dong Ha for lunch.

After lunch, we paid a visit to Project RENEW that is working to reduce the number of deaths and injuries caused by cluster bombs and other munitions remaining in Quang Tri Province since the war ended. We also toured the House of Exhibits showing the devastation of the Vietnam War, its consequences, and the recovery from loss, pains, and poverty by the people.

Thereafter, we continued the drive with a short stop at the demilitarized zone before driving two hours further to Hue city. We walked across the bridge at the DMZ. I got my picture taken with one foot in the former South Vietnam and my other foot in the former North Vietnam.

We arrived in Hue at half past five and checked into the EMM hotel. We had dinner at the nearby Moc Vien restaurant. Thao was born in Hue city and was staying overnight at her parents' home.

After breakfast the next day, we went by bus to Tinh Truc Gia (Peaceful Bamboo Family Center), an organization that approaches, educates, and creates livable environments for people with mental disabilities. We visited their bio garden, teahouse, vocational classes, and had a nice vegetarian lunch with the staff and patients. After lunch, we went by bus to the nearby Thien Mu pagoda, followed by taking a boat downstream on the Perfume River to city central. There, we visited the Minh Mang Tomb and the Citadel. Then we went back to the hotel for some free time before dinner at the La Carambole restaurant.

On Thursday after breakfast, we left Hue for a three-hour bus ride to Da Nang. On the way, we went over Hai Van Pass with beautiful tree-covered mountains everywhere and later had short stops to visit Lang Co Beach and Marble Mountain. In Da Nang, we visited a local family and enjoyed a warm home-cooked meal with the host family. The owner of the house was a chef, and he and his parents, wife, and daughter prepared the meal. Their two-story house had roomy living and dining rooms, kitchen, and office and three bedrooms upstairs. After lunch, we continued our drive and arrived in Hoi An town an hour later.

Hoi An was voted one of the top 10 cities in Asia one year by Travel. *The old town forms a big part of the city's appeal. Listed as a UNESCO World Heritage Site, the old town is compact and walkable, boasting preserved buildings on streets covered with cascading flowers. Every month on the night of the full moon, people in the old town celebrate the moon deity and limit their use of electricity so one can bask in the beautiful glow of hundreds of lanterns. There are also numerous dinner cruises down Thu Bon River from this charming old trading port.*

At two, we checked into the Venus hotel, had a two-hour rest, and then visited the Hoi An daily market. In the evening, we walked about half a mile, through lots of traffic while watching for breaks in the sidewalks and scooters whizzing by, to a large walking street on both sides of a river. In the pier area, we walked through a long-covered bridge, one side built by Chinese merchants and the other side by Japanese merchants. There were many shops selling a wide variety of things on both sides of the pier as well as many docked boats of various sizes.

We had the next day in Hoi An to do whatever we wanted. I chose to work on my diary, write postcards, edit pictures in my camera, get a wonderful massage at the hotel, and have a long walk before dinner at seven.

We had an early breakfast at the hotel the next morning followed by a bus ride to the Da Nang airport for our Vietnam Airways flight to Saigon (Ho Chi Minh City). The Da Nang airport has separate domestic and international terminals. The domestic terminal has ten gates, and there were many tourists boarding numerous flights.

Upon arrival in bustling Saigon, we met our new local guide and driver and then headed out to untouched areas not well-known by tourists in Ben Tre. After enjoying a lunch served with Mekong specialties, we took a rowboat ride through winding canals. Back on shore, we visited a local village to enjoy tea with honey, meet some local families, and see how local traditional methods utilize every bit of the coconut. At half past four, we left Ben Tre for Saigon City, arriving an hour later. After checking in at the Le Duy Hotel, we had dinner at the classy Chopsticks restaurant.

Following breakfast on Sunday at the hotel, we went on a city sightseeing tour, visiting the depressing war museum (with pictures showing the tragic effects Agent Orange and napalm had on the population), Reunification Palace, French Colonial building on Dong Khoi Street, Post Office (where there were many souvenir shops), and Ben Thanh Market. After lunch, we went to Tan Son Nhat International Airport for our four in the afternoon departure flight. The international terminal is new and has twenty-eight gates and lots of shops.

Several weeks after his return to his old life, James receives a letter from Deborah:

Dear Richard, I mean James (ha ha),

I know you have at least four other names besides Richard and James: John, Johnny, Jim, and Jimmy. What are the others? I hope this letter finds you well and enjoying the resumption of your life with your family and job. I wrote this letter after my return from our trip together but waited to mail it since I was not sure about contacting you. After we went our separate ways in Santiago, I went onto Cusco and Machu Picchu, both UNESCO World Heritage Sites, in hope it would ease the pain of losing you. It did help a little since the trip was great with one exciting part. The day after you departed, I flew to Cusco via Lima. The city was the historic capital of the Inca Empire from the thirteenth to the sixteenth century. After my arrival at a first-class hotel, and since Cusco is 11,000 feet in elevation, I started drinking lots of Coca tea, which is supposed to help with altitude sickness. I spent the first full day wondering around the beautiful city with its Inca and Spanish colonial buildings. I especially liked Sacsayhuaman, the Inca Ceremonial Fortress, with its stacks of beautiful large boulders of all shapes and sizes stacked tightly together. One wonders how the Incas crafted the large blocks. The greatest thing about dinner that night at the hotel restaurant was drinking a couple of Pisco Sours. They are sure good!

Early the following day, I went to Machu Picchu via army helicopter since a bad rainstorm had washed out the train tracks in places. The ride was quite exciting and was the first time I was in a helicopter. Machu Picchu, a fifteenth-century Inca citadel, is breathtaking and in excellent shape. I greatly enjoyed walking through its three primary structures, Intihuatana, Temple of the Sun, and Room of the Three Windows. Most of the outlying buildings have been restored. It was fun and interesting, although the altitude was starting to get me in the afternoon. In the evening, I helicoptered back to Cusco for the night and returned home the next morning. I miss you. Please stay in touch.

Love, Deborah

Near Christmas, Deborah received a card from James that included a summary of his activities and holiday plans. He also wrote that his children are coming to Pendleton to spend an early Christmas with him and Ying. They are both excited about their visit since they do not see much of them these days.

A few weeks later, James receives another letter from Deborah:

Dear James,

I hope you are well and now completely settled down in your old life. I am missing you so much. One thing you did for me was to renew my interest in traveling. On that note, I just returned from a trip to Ecuador. My good friend Coni, whom you met in Santiago, invited me to go on the three-week trip that was sponsored by Global Exchange, a humanitarian, nonprofit organization located in San Francisco. I took your advice and started keeping a diary. The following is what I wrote about this trip:

The Ecuador adventure began with an overnight flight from Santiago to Quito, arriving midmorning. After landing, we took a taxi to the Ikala Hotel. Following check-in, we met our delegation leader, Yuri, in the hotel lobby, along with our two traveling companions, Will from Ohio and Gusta from Brazil. Yuri told us he was sick, food poisoning from eating fish soup the night before. Also, there was a loud party in the house next door that kept him awake all night. I suggested to Yuri that he go home and spend the day in bed. He agreed and arranged for another guide to host us the next day.

Our new guide, Louis, arrived after breakfast, along with a driver and Mercedes van. We went through busy, sprawling Quito with a population of two million. There were lots of vendors selling a variety of goods at stoplights, and many homes are located on the mountainsides. In leaving the city, we went past a monument marking the "Middle of the World" and then traveled about an hour to Yunguilla Village, high on a hill surrounded by several beautiful mountain ranges. Louis, who lives in the village with his wife and four children, told us the 10,000-acre area was divided in the 1960s for the people working the land. During that time, the workers were mainly making moonshine from sugarcane and clearing the forest for firewood and growing crops. Now the community of fifteen families is organized around self-sustainability and protectors of the cloud forest. We heard from the village leader about their various projects and that *now their main income is from organic farming and tourism. There are several volunteers coming each year, mainly from the Netherlands, to help in the fields and plant fast-growing trees. We were shown a large and lovely vegetable garden surrounded by fruit trees, and nearby were a few cows and horses. After a late lunch of soup and pizza, we started our return to the city. On the way, our group exchanged some information about themselves. I gave my usual narrative about being a retired medical doctor who lives on Navarino Island, Chile. Coni also said she was a medical doctor but still practicing in Santiago. Gusta told us a little about his city and job. One thing that stood out was hearing about his mountain climbing; he has climbed Rucu Pichincha Mountain, 15,000 feet, after riding part way in a chairlift. Will is also a mountain climber and has spent lots of vacation time in Ecuador. In fact, he was in Quito when the country had its major financial crisis and changed their currency from the Sucre to the U.S. dollar. They do, however, mint their own coins. During this time, Will bought an upscale condo in Quito for $24,000.*

The next day, with gray skies and a little rain, we started our five-hour drive to the city of Puyo on the major highway going from one end of the country to the other. The speed limit is sixty miles per hour. The road goes through a large valley with mountains on both sides lined with grass and trees. Part way, the highway paralleled the Windy River. Most of the cars on the road were Chevrolets since they are manufactured in Quito. There were many people along the road, either selling their goods in their roadside shacks or waiting for their bus. Some of the roadside vendors were selling a variety of life-size stuffed dolls and animals to be burned on New Year's Eve, a traditional custom. Most of the houses in the small towns we passed were made from concrete or cinder block. About halfway, we had lunch at Mondel Swiss Bistro in the nice little tourist city of Banos with views of a volcano in the distance. Following our arrival in Puyo, we had meetings with several indigenous leaders of the city. In the evening, we had dinner at the hotel El Jardin, where we spent the night. Coni and I shared a room.

Following breakfast at the hotel and checking out, we had a short ride to the small airport in the adjoining town of Shell. There we took a half-hour flight in a six-seater, one-engine plane to Sarayacu. The view on the ride was mostly of rolling hills and rainforest. The landing was quite scary as the landing/takeoff runway was short, and only half of it was paved; the other half was gravel and dirt. We were met by a small crowd of village families that included some beautiful two- to five-year-old children.

After greeting the crowd in the hot weather, the five of us were transported up the Bobonaza River, about a mile, in a motorized canoe to our host's home. The home has a large guest hut that has six rooms with beds covered with mosquito nets. We did not see any mosquitos but heard bats flying over the nets at night. The walls of the straw-covered building are only waist high with the upper half open to the outside with no windows. The area under the building is open, and one goes up a flight of stairs to get to the bedrooms. Of course, there is no electricity, only candlelight and bottled propane for cooking. They use walkie-talkies for communication within the village and surroundings. Our host has a wife, baby boy, and four beautiful girls, one a teenager and the other three under six years old. We had a great time during our stay playing with the three youngsters. The older girl helped her mother with the meals. There was also a cow, donkey, three dogs, a wild cat, and lots of chickens on the acre property. The cat was very funny as he chased the dogs and chickens around. There were many kinds of butterflies but few birds and wildlife in or near the home.

After lunch, we had the first of several meetings with the village leaders. The villagers are trying to protect their land from oil drilling, logging, and mining. During the past forty years, a Norway company had been taking oil without giving the people any payment, even though they own the land. In 2000, there was an uprising against the government to make the drilling stop; the villagers were successful. They are also against the government wanting to put roads into their properties since they think companies will come and destroy their sacred land by taking their natural resources. We were also told that the village survives on farming, fishing, and tourism.

On New Year's Eve, after being woken by drumbeating, a nice breakfast was served. Later in the day, most of the villagers met at a community area that has a school, meeting rooms, and other buildings. One thing they did in the evening was to pass around a large bowl of a traditional drink containing alcohol, followed by a delightful meal. Later, there was a wonderful celebration with music and dancing.

The following two days were spent having further meetings with indigenous leaders, going on some small hikes wearing borrowed rubber boots through the rainforest on muddy trails, and visits to different beautiful places. It had rained on all the nights during our visit but not during the day.

We left by plane for Shell on the last morning of the adventure then by van back to Quito, a 120-mile ride. We returned to the same hotel that we had stayed the first two nights.

The next day, we made an hour trip to the province of Cotopaxi to visit the highland indigenous community and to have meetings with their leaders. Following the meetings, we went into the large Cotopaxi National Park. There, we visited the park's museum. Afterward, we had a nice lunch at the park restaurant called Hosteria Tambopaxi, two thousand feet above sea level, with views of several volcanoes, including the snowcapped Volcan Cotopaxi, at nineteen thousand feet. In the late afternoon, we returned to our hotel and later had a nice goodbye dinner.

On the last morning of the trip, we said my goodbyes to Will, Gusta, and Yuri and got on a flight back to Santiago, where I spent a couple of nights with Coni before going home.

Love and best wishes, Deborah

James wrote back, inviting her to come to Clemson when possible so he can introduce her to Ying and their friends and show her around South Carolina.

James's new office and research laboratories are on the fourth floor of the Hunter Chemistry Building that is located about the middle of campus. The first floor of the building has general chemistry laboratories, the second floor some teaching and administrative rooms, the third a mix of teaching and research laboratories, and the top floor mostly research laboratories.

Besides a secretary and small staff, James supervises a dozen faculty members, including Ying. He also has two new graduate students and will teach an actinide chemistry class in the fall.

James and Ying usually drive their own cars to campus, James in a Chevy convertible and Ying in Margrit's Smart car. They both take the steep and curvy Queen Street out of Pendleton. Ying's office and laboratory are on the second floor of the Hunter Building, and she and James usually meet for lunch in the nearby campus restaurant. If Ying does not prepare dinner, they go into Pendleton's old town square, where there are several restaurants, including the Plantation House.

One warm and sunny morning, the Czermaks leave the Smart car at Rick's garage for two days of repairs. Then they both go to work in James's convertible with the top down. After arrival in the parking lot, James discovers that the convertible top will not go up. So they leave the car in the parking lot all day with the top down. At the end of the workday, James phones Ying and tells her that he needs to work late. He recommends that she go home for dinner and that he will call her for a ride home when he finishes his work. It had just gotten dark as Ying goes to the parking lot and starts driving James's car home.

Several hours later, James tries to call Ying without success. While he is waiting to reach her by phone, he turns on his office television to hear the local news. The first story was about a hit-and-run accident near Pendleton on Queen Street. They show a burned-out and upside-down Chevy convertible down in a ravine surrounded by trees, with a fire truck and several police cars on the road. James hysterically jumps as he recognizes his car. The newsman reports that the driver burned to death and that the accident is under investigation. With tears in his eyes, James frantically calls the police about the accident. He tells the operator that it was his wife who died in the car crash on Queen Street and that someone should come to his building to take him to the tragic accident scene. After arriving at the accident site by police car, James is informed that the remains of the driver are only ashes, and they found the hit-and-run vehicle, a large pickup that had been stolen earlier in Anderson.

An anguished James did not get any sleep that night and found out in the morning that the fire was started with a Molotov cocktail and that the flames ignited the gas tank. The police now concludes that Ying was murdered. James spends the morning wondering who would want to kill Ying. She was liked and loved by everyone who knew her. But did she have an enemy back in China who came to South Carolina to kill her?

With tears in his eyes, James makes a few difficult phone calls to his children, Ying's daughter, and several close friends to inform them of Ying's tragic death. He also tells the dean that he will need to take a week or so away from campus to arrange a memorial for her. The dreadful time he had after Margrit's death was reoccurring.

Ying and James's families come to the funeral as well as many friends, fellow faculty members, and students. They have a wonderful memorial. The following day, James sends out the following e-mail:

> *Dear family and friends,*
>
> *Thank you so much for your thoughtful cards and e-mails on the passing of Ying. I received almost fifty e-mails and cards of condolences from loved ones and friends, and over twenty people attended her funeral and memorial. Your cards and/or presence at the memorial gave me much comfort. Of course, it was great to see Ying's daughter, who came all the way from Vancouver, Canada, with her family. Ying was loved by many people. Her memorial letter is attached.*
>
> *Love and best wishes, John James Czermak*

III

On a cold and windy Saturday night, it is unusual to find anyone in the chemistry building. Earlier, Czermak had been showing his graduate student, Igor Medvedev, how to operate the gas chromatograph/mass spectrometer systems. Now he is performing his own experiment with the instrument. So engrossed with the analysis, he is unaware that behind him, the laboratory door has opened. An unseen hand tosses a Molotov cocktail into the room, which explodes at once, shooting flames in every direction. The sea of flames creates an inferno, and within seconds, fire is licking at James's feet and legs. Poisonous fumes have permeated the air, blinding, chocking, and disorienting him.

As he is crawling across the laboratory floor, he now knows for certain that the car crash that killed Ying was meant for him, just like the raging inferno around him. James manages to crawl to one of the windows, opens it, and jumps from the ledge to a nearby tree. After climbing to the ground, he sees a man running toward the street. James dashes after him but barely gets to the car as it is pulling away. James does get a good look at the driver and remembers the car and license plate number. Several minutes after calling 911, a fire truck arrives, along with two police cars.

After the fire is out, the police captain arrives and asks James to come to the nearby police station for questioning. At the station, James tells the captain all he knows about the fire, including his conclusion that someone is trying to kill him. Then the captain got a report on the assassin's car. It was a stolen car and was just found abandoned in Anderson just like the truck that killed his wife. They should be able to get fingerprints in the car to match up with the ones obtained from the stolen truck. However, the fingerprints in the truck did not match any in police or FBI files.

Chapter 4
More Travels

I

One day James hears a knock on his office door. He goes to the door and finds a lady who looks a little like Marilyn Monroe. He invites her into his office. After he shuts the door, she pulls out her credentials and introduces herself. "I am CIA Agent Kim Carn and have replaced retired Agent Tim Smith as your contact. I know he told you that another agent would be contacting you for your continued assistance to the CIA. I am so sorry to hear about your accident in Chile, the loss of your wife, and now the fire and attempts on your life. Is this a good time to discuss how you can continue to assist us?"

"Yes, I have some time now."

"First, here is a copy of my business card for you. As you can see, it only has my name on it, and of course, Kim Carn is not my real name. I have read the large file we have on you, and I was also briefed by Tim before he retired. You deserve a big thanks for all the work you did for us in the past. However, I want to know if you are still willing to take some government-paid trips, some that could be dangerous, to obtain certain information for us, mostly about nuclear weapons proliferation."

James agreed to cooperate and serve his country as best he could.

"Your CIA assignment on your trip to Antarctica over a year ago was to find out if someone aboard ship was passing nuclear weapons information to a small group of nuclear scientists from the Argentinean Nuclear Energy Agency. During the past year, we have obtained enough information to conclude that Argentina was not trying to develop the bomb, but now Brazil is suspect.

Thus, we would like you to take a trip to visit your friend at the Brazilian Atomic Energy site in São Paulo and find out all you can about their possible involvement with nuclear weapons. We know you have been to the site before as an IAEA expert, and you reported that you saw a secure area where uranium enrichment was taking place. You are welcome to use this trip to visit your friend who saved your life on Cape Horn."

"If you approve, I will also use the trip to visit a couple of South American countries I have never been to before."

"Certainly, that is okay."

"Thank you. The reason that I want to try and visit some countries I have not been to before is because I am a member of the Traveler's Century Club, and the club has a list of 327 countries and territories that members are recommended to visit." He then tells Kim more about the club.

At the end of the meeting, Kim swore James to secrecy, never to discuss their meetings, CIA assignments, or relationship with her to anyone, just like he had done for Tim.

II

Travel funds arrive for James two weeks later from the Penny Group in San Francisco, CIA's financial front. The day after explaining to the dean that he needed some travel time to give an invited talk in Brazil as well as spend some vacation time in South America that may help him overcome the loss of Ying, he drives to the Atlanta airport. As he is waiting to catch the subway to the international terminal, a good-looking young lady gets off the train, looks at James, and says, "Hello, John. I remember you from the Habitat for Humanity trip to the Dominican Republic."

"Katelin, what a small world to see you here."

"John, you have not changed a bit these many years, still handsome as ever. That was sure two weeks of hard work, building the cinder brick home in that small Dominican Republic village for the family of six living in a shack."

"Yes, the project was a great experience, and it was rewarding to see the mother with her five young children move into the new home. I do not think today that I could carry two cinder blocks at a time for those many days."

"John, I am sorry, but I need to get to the gate to catch my flight to Los Angeles. It was great to see you. Goodbye and take care."

After a departing hug, James waves as she is running to her gate.

On the flight from Atlanta to Santiago, James had the aisle seat, and the middle seat was vacant. The young lady at the window introduced herself to James. Sara had just graduated from Florida State University with a degree in astronomy. She was heading to Machu Picchu to walk the Inca Trail in three days. She said that she would be meeting other friends there and that they had a guide who would bring tents and camping gear. In the fall, she will start a PhD program in astronomy at Columbia University. Her goal is to be an astrophysicist and professor.

James asked her, "Do you know Professor Karl Chopen?"

"Well, everyone at the university knows of this famous professor of chemistry. I took his course and loved it because of his interesting style of lecturing. He always put several jokes in his talks."

After arriving in Puerto Williams via Santiago and Punta Arenas, James is met by Deborah in the small arrivals hall of the airport. She is overjoyed to see him, and they both go to her car after a loving embrace. On the drive, she tells James how sorry she is about Ying's tragic death. They both exchange stories about some of their activities since James left Chile many months ago. After the couple arrive at Deborah's home, Mary and Eduardo come over for a wonderful reunion. Later over dinner, James tells Deborah about his trip to see her, his plans to go to Brazil, and more about his life in South Carolina.

"Deb, since my memory has almost completely returned, I will tell you some major things about my life, some of which I have told you before after our meeting with Durado in Trujillo. Over a decade ago, I spent three years at the International Atomic Energy Agency in Vienna, Austria. Before then, I worked at the Rocky Flats Plant, near Denver, Colorado, where triggers for nuclear weapons are made. In my previous work at the plant, I was a major contributor to the development of the neutron bomb. In Vienna, KGB agents were trying to get information for the bomb from me via Margrit, my first wife, who became romantically involved with Andrei Pushkin, thought by the CIA to be a KGB agent. Realizing the futility of their relationship, Margrit told me about Andrei and how they both had on several occasions unsuccessfully attempted to terminate it. Later, Andrei committed suicide, and Margrit was beside herself with grief, but that event saved our marriage. Later, I was to find out that Andrei had faked his suicide and left Vienna for Canada to start a new life. After leaving the agency, Margrit and I returned to our home in Arvada, Colorado, and resumed a close, loving relationship that had been severely damaged in Vienna. I also returned to my former job at Rocky Flats as manager of Plutonium Chemistry Research and Development.

"About this time, I traveled a lot to conferences around the world and to Vienna and Moscow to have meetings with my two Russian coauthors on a series of books we were writing for the IAEA. Following more contacts with my Russian colleagues, I was informed that a background investigation had been conducted by the Department of Energy and the FBI. This investigation resulted in losing my security clearance. I then went to Australia to teach for three years and later to work in California for three years. Andrei came to California and tried to renew his relationship with Margrit and kill me, but instead, he accidentally killed Margrit. I found out later that he committed suicide in Canada and told his son, Alex, in his dying breath that I had shot him.

"At that point, I wanted to start a new life and left California for a teaching job at Clemson University. I even started using my middle name. I enjoyed the academic life very much, supervising several students and teaching actinide chemistry. I even purchased the car and home that Margrit liked. The automobile is a small Smart car, and the home has three bedrooms upstairs and two downstairs with bathrooms in all the bedrooms, plus living and dining rooms, and kitchens on both floors. I rent the basement to two graduate students in my department.

"Alex joined my research group using a different last name. I did not know that he was Andrei's youngest son. In early January, I took him, Ying, Shana, and another student of mine with me on an expedition to Antarctica, where we would do some ice sampling. By that time, I had fallen in love with Ying. We were married by the ship's captain as we crossed the Antarctic Circle. The following night, me, Alex, and a dozen other brave souls camped out on Hovgaard Island, where I had an attempt on my life. On the last night of the trip, as we were crossing the Drake Passage and heading past Cape Horn, the sea was very rough, and large waves were coming over the front of the ship. Alex met me at the stern of the ship and with difficulty admitted that his real name was Alexander Pushkin, that his father was the one who had a love affair with Margrit in Vienna, and that his father had cut the break lines on my car in California with the intention of killing me and not Margrit. I was shocked as Alex admitted that on the camping night, it was he who had kicked the rock that was holding me and my sleeping bag in place. As I was sliding down the hill, Alex told me that he was immediately sorry for what he had done and ran trying to stop me but that I had managed to stop myself at the edge of the hill. His father shot himself in his home in Canada where Alex was staying, and his father told him in his dying breath that I had shot him and that he should kill me. I sternly told Alex that I did not kill his father and have an alibi. Alex agreed and told me he learned that morning that his father had committed suicide. Alex told me that he was extremely sorry that he had tried to kill me. At the end of our conversation, I told Alex that under the circumstances, I forgive him. My last words were for him to come and give me a big bear hug. Alex happily jumped over and gave me an embrace that caused both of us to accidentally fall over the back of the ship into the rough, freezing ocean."

After finishing dinner, James tells Deborah how much he has missed her and that a day does not go by without him thinking of her. He then takes her in his arms and gives her a long romantic kiss. Following the embrace, James says, "If you agree, someday I would like to marry you, but first, I must find out who is trying to kill me so that you do not come into harm's way. I told the authorities that one of my students is a Russian, but I have no reason why he would desire to kill me. The only other persons I thought would want me dead would be Andrei's eldest son and/ or his uncle since they might think I killed both Andrei and Alex. The FBI did go through government records and reviewed the names of all visiting Russians the past year, but there were no Pushkins on the list."

"James, I love you so much, and of course, I want to marry you. It would be a dream come true." The couple continue to talk until bedtime, where James is invited into Deborah's room for the night.

The next morning, James asks Deborah if she would like to come with him to Brazil and maybe visit some other nearby countries as well. Of course, she agrees and starts making arrangements to join him on a flight to São Paulo via Punta Arenas and Santiago the next day.

III

During the flight from Santiago to São Paulo, James tells Deborah about his second time to Brazil when he attended a nuclear conference in Maresias, a small tourist town next to the

South Atlantic Ocean. He also relates to her about some other South American trips.

"As you know, São Paulo is a large city, stretching out for miles to house its ten million inhabitants. After arriving in São Paulo, I boarded a bus to Maresias. The bus ride took four hours, and the highway went from eight lanes to four lanes to two lanes. The curvy two-lane road went through beautiful tree-covered hills and mountains. There were lots of palm and banana trees and even an incredibly beautiful waterfall dropping from a mountaintop to the valley below. As the bus got close to the South Atlantic Ocean, I could see a beautiful island in the distance and wonderful beaches with lots of sunbathers and swimmers. We went through one big city and then several small towns with dirt side streets. Most of the houses in the towns were made from cinder blocks, and a lot of them were partly built but still lived in. After reaching Maresias, the bus stopped in front of the Beach Hotel, and guess what, it faced the beach, but I did not get a beachfront room but one near the main road going through Maresias.

"Late on Sunday afternoon, I took a walk on the beach before the reception of the conference. There were lots of sunbathers, swimmers, and surfers around. The Fourth International Nuclear Chemistry Congress was held across the street from the hotel in a conference building. I was one of twenty International Scientific Board members. Margrit and I had attended the second such conference in Cancun, Mexico, years ago.

"There was a conference opening ceremony that night, followed by a reception. At the social, I met some of my friends that I have known many years. Of course, Cecee, who you will meet in São Paulo, was there. I have known her the longest, and the last time we were together was at a conference in Hawaii, where Margrit was with me. The first time was when I was in São Paulo as an IAEA expert to visit her nuclear research site and advise Cecee how to process americium contained on the tips of used lightning rods.

"In Maresias, I attended talks all day on Monday with all the attendees, including Cecee, Ana, and a couple of their fellow workers. In the evening before dinner, I had a nice walk around the little village of Maresias. The weather was great. It was hard to believe it was winter in the U.S. The small town has lots of hotels and restaurants, and the main road through town parallels the beach. There were more presentations the next day at the conference.

"Wednesday was a free day, and I took an excursion with ten other conference attendees via speedboat to Ilhabela Island. It is about sixty miles around the beautiful island, and the population is about ten thousand. The occupants used to grow and export coffee, sugarcane, and bananas, but now they rely mostly on tourism and fishing. In the early days, slaves were imported to cut the sugarcane.

"After arriving at a town called No Name, we had a wet boarding on a Flex boat and about an hour rough ride on the ocean to the farthest place we would visit on the island, a cove called Eustaguio, with four houses. On the way over, we had seen a whale, and a little later, the driver stopped the boat, and our guide asked if everyone was feeling okay on the wild ride. I then pretended like I was vomiting and got some laughs from my fellow passengers. At the cove, we had some snacks and climbed an embankment using a rope to see the bay on the other side. There was a young boy and a much younger beautiful girl playing on the beach and a small kiosk with drinks for sale. A few of the folks swam, and the couple from the Netherlands snorkeled. The rest of the group just sat around talking during the hour's stay.

"On the return to port, the driver went a little slower and stopped at several small beach areas with a few houses. I commented to the guide that it must have been expensive to bring the building materials in by boat. The driver said in broken English that most of the wood as well as the rocks were obtained from the island. One small community had a small school. Our guide told us that in the small village, there were several big rocks that made loud noises if you hit them hard. This phenomenon later saved the people one night in the past from an attacking group of pirates to ward off their surprise attack. We were also told that there was a shipwreck nearby many decades ago. The ship had the same design as the *Titanic* and was built by the same company in Belfast, Ireland. All were lost aboard the ship, but its sinking was not nearly as known as the *Titanic* disaster. When our group returned to No Name, we had lunch and a short walk around the city center then returned to the conference center by bus.

"In the evening following dinner, there was the same singer-guitar player we had on Monday, but this time the lady that controlled the meeting accompanied him singing. She was great, and Ana also joined her for a couple of songs. At the end, the lady asked us if we wanted to come up, one at a time, and sing a song representing our country's culture. First, she said how about someone from the U.S.? Since I was sitting in the front table with Ana, she and the rest of the audience urged me to get up and sing a song. Reluctantly, I got up and did a wonderful dancing and singing rendition of Elvis's 'Hound Dog.' My performance was a big hit as I also had the audience singing, wailing, and clapping during the end. Several other conference attendees also sang some good songs representative of their country."

"James, I did not know you were so talented, but of course, I have always enjoyed your humor."

"Part of the lady singer's job during the conference was to give the speaker a note that read 'One minute left.' As the singer was thanking us at the end, I passed her a note with 'One minute left' written on it. She laughed and told the audience of my antic, and everyone had a final good laugh.

"The next morning, she told me that her dad was a successful singer, and he did not want his daughter to follow him in his footsteps. Thus, he encouraged her to go into business studies that included running conferences.

"After the closing ceremony, I left for the San Pedro airport via bus. The ride back seemed more spectacular. The jungle-covered mountains, some trees with flowers, and the high and long waterfall made the four-hour ride seem much shorter."

"James, that sure sounds like a wonderful trip and a great conference."

"As part of that trip, I made a short visit to Asuncion, Paraguay. The flight from São Paulo to Asuncion was two hours. I stayed at the four-star International Hotel Asuncion, but it was more like a rundown three-star American motel. The first night there was a loud fireworks event, followed by a parade of noisy people and loud music in cars. I was told the next morning that they were celebrating the end of winter.

"After breakfast, I went for about a two-hour walk around the downtown center of Asuncion. The city has some beautiful architecture, old and new buildings. Some of the old ones were abandoned and decayed. There was a large slum area between the Paraguay River and the new and modern House of Congress. The slum homes, probably fifty of them, were one-room shacks made from plywood. There were a few portable toilets throughout the community. The area was about two blocks by six blocks. I saw some beautiful children that were playing, and they looked happy despite their circumstances. The palace was also pleasant to look at, but I keep wondering about its name, Gobierno. Since the German word for beer is 'bier,' the palace might have been named 'go, beer, no!'"

Deborah laughs and says, "You are indeed a comedian."

"The other notable buildings were Iglesia Cathedral, the House of Independence, Place of the National Heroes, and the Catholic University.

"In the afternoon, I went out again to explore another part of the city center. It was Sunday, and few folks were out, and the shops were closed. People came out in the afternoon for dining, and I saw only four foreigners. All the streets were one way, and there were only a few stop signs and two stoplights. Most of the sidewalks in the city center were damaged, and I had to be careful in maneuvering around. There were lots of police everywhere, including outside the restaurants.

"The next morning, I took a taxi to the airport. The Asuncion airport is quite nice and not too big—four gates all leading off from a small waiting area with coffee and duty-free shops. Airport security was excellent, but they confiscated my hand disinfectant unlike many other airports that I have gone through with it. On the flight to São Paulo, I remember blue skies, great weather, and the land below the plane was flat with lots of nice green pastures and farms."

IV

The couple arrived at the São Paulo airport, where James's Brazilian friend, Cecee, and her husband, Walt, greeted them. The foursome then went to Cecee and Walt's home for a late dinner, where they got caught up on one another's past several years of activities.

Following a night of restful sleep at their host's home and an early morning breakfast, the foursome went to see the interesting sites in the city. After lunch, Deborah and Walt continued the city tour, while Cecee and James went to her institute for James to give an invited lecture. After the seminar, Cecee took James on a tour of the research laboratories and the institute's nuclear center. The center has an experimental nuclear power reactor and an area where uranium enrichment research is being performed. On the way back to Cecee and Walt's home, James candidly asked her about activities relating to building a nuclear weapon somewhere at her institute. She assured him that no such activities were taking place, and there is no intention of the government undertaking such a project. She continued. "If there were any efforts to build a bomb, my colleagues and I would know about it. Furthermore, I think if Brazil had the bomb, some other South American countries would do the same thing, especially Venezuela."

After three nights in São Paulo, James and Deborah fly to Buenos Aires. During the flight, James tells Deborah about a trip he made to Morocco and Mali.

"The North African adventure started in Casablanca, following my flight from London. Casablanca is an interesting city of seven million people. On my only day there, I had a walk around the old city center to see the main and historic sites. There is even a 'Rick's Café,' like the one in the movie *Casablanca* with Humphrey Bogart, where I had lunch. The movie is one of my favorites. I especially like what Rick said a couple of times when toasting to Ilsa with a drink: 'Here's looking at you, kid.' Have you seen the movie?"

"Yes, of course. I also love the movie, especially Sam's singing 'As Time Goes By' and his piano playing."

"Early the next morning, I was awakened by the call to prayer. Thus, I caught an earlier train to Marrakesh. On the trip, we passed through several small towns, all between lots of green farmland with roaming cattle. Following my arrival in Marrakesh, I checked into the nice Ibis hotel. Across the street from the hotel is a large and beautiful opera house.

"At breakfast the next day, there was a guy playing the piano, and one of the songs he played surprised me. It was 'Santa Claus Is Coming to Town.' Later, I took a horse and buggy ride through the old walled city and saw many interesting buildings. A large mosque was the main attraction. In the afternoon, I took a bus tour outside the old city. Marrakesh is very modern with many new buildings. On the two tours, I saw many lovely people walking about and beautiful children playing. In general, the people seem very well-off, but there was a significant amount of people asking for money, especially elderly women and mothers with babies.

"After two nights in Marrakech, I boarded a train back to Casablanca and then transferred to another train to Tangier. The ride to Tangier was spectacular. The land was very green with lots of small lakes, wheat and grass fields, wildlife, birds, farm animals, and small villages with many people slowly building their half-completed homes. Rolling hills appeared during the last hour of the ride. I stayed at the Ibis hotel for two nights.

"Following a late breakfast the next day, I had a walk around the old city and then back to the hotel along the beach. The old city was interesting. After lunch, I went on another beach walk in the opposite direction of the morning walk and saw that there were lots of new construction in this part of the city and a circus next to the train station featuring tigers who were in small cages.

"We should start a campaign for a worldwide boycott of circuses and zoos, where all the innocent animals are caged. They need their natural wide-open spaces, which game reserves and national parks can provide. When you come to the U.S., I will take you to the Wild Animal Sanctuary near Denver, Colorado."

"That sounds great, and I agree with you that wild animals need their freedom."

"Tangier is certainly not catering to tourism as in Marrakesh, which has lots of American fast-food places and clean and modern restaurants. Casablanca is in between these two cities in amenities. I had not seen any tourists, and the hotel seems to have only a few businessmen staying there.

"I had hoped to take a ferry to Gibraltar, but it did not work out, so I returned to Casablanca for the night. The next morning, I took the train to their airport for my flight to the capital of Mali. Bamako is located on the banks of the Niger River. That waterway flows for hundreds of miles winding through the savanna of West Africa, eventually emptying into the ocean. It serves as the main channel for travel and commerce in the whole sub-Saharan area. But Bamako itself is very unimpressive in appearance and functionality, even though it is home to almost two million people.

"Following my arrival in Bamako, I left for Mopi with twelve passengers and two pilots on a two-propeller Air Mali plane.

The flight to Mopi was a little over an hour. After arrival, all the passengers got off except me. The two pilots then flew me to Timbuktu in about two hours.

"The legendary city of Timbuktu was the ancient crossroads where camel caravans carrying gold, salt, and slaves from the black kingdoms in the south connected with the Arab sheikdoms to the north. The local Tuareg people led the convoys, and Timbuktu became wealthy as the center of trade. Eventually, it declined in importance as ships supplying the coastline proved more efficient. The town still boasts the largest mud structure in the world, which serves as a huge inn and meeting place, although it does dry out and must be reconstructed every other year.

"I was met at the Timbuktu airport at noon and taken to the Grand Hotel, the only hotel in the town, by Mohammed, my driver, and Sani, my guide, in a white Toyota Land Cruiser with four-wheel drive. On the ride to the hotel, Sani told me he plants trees in the summer when the tourist business stops. I was the only guest at the thirty-room hotel. The hotel manager said business had been bad since the French tourists were kidnapped a few months ago. That night, I had a restless sleep since I was the only guest in the hotel, and I kept thinking of the movie *The Shining* with Jack Nicholson."

"James, that hotel sounds like the same one we stayed at in Patagonia."

"You are right. The next day, I visited four mosques, the museum, library, post office, and big and small shopping areas. People are nice and friendly but extremely poor. They mainly raise livestock and transport items down the Niger River.

"The third day, I went by camel, with the white Toyota following, to visit a Tuareg village on the dunes. The village was easily reached by camel and is where the villagers raise goats and some cattle. I was told that it was too dangerous to go further out into the desert because of Al-Qaeda. At the camp, I was introduced to a local Tuareg chief. He was quite tall, dressed in the traditional deep blue robe, and his smiling face had a dark olive complexion. He told me in perfect English how he spent two years at the University of Colorado, where most people assumed he was Mexican. Although there was now a paved road across the Sahara, he informed me that he still leads camel caravans from the desert salt mines to the urban centers. The continuing success of the ancient mode of transport, he said, was because trucks get stuck when the blowing sand clogs their engines or large dunes block the road. Other people told me later that the camels would soon be outdated, but I prefer to believe that our Tuareg chieftain will be leading his caravans for years to come.

"The Tuareg camp elders offered me tea and then asked me very cautiously if they could show me their goods, mainly jewelry wrapped up in cloth. I told them I did not need anything. They kept saying the money would help the camp, and the people are so poor, and tourism was ending with the increased hot weather, and the coming rainy season lasts until August or September. Before I left, I gave them some money.

"On my last morning there, I went to the airport with Mohammed and Sani. I left Timbuktu on the same Air Mali plane I arrived in, and after a stop in Mopti, the plane landed before noon in Bamako. There, I took a tour around the city. Bamako is nice, and there are big roundabouts, also known as traffic circles, on their main streets. One roundabout had a statue of a hippo in the middle, an elephant in another traffic circle, and animals of different kinds in other circles. After the tour, I walked around an open market and witnessed how they treat animals. One guy was holding six live turkeys in each hand by their legs and was swinging them wildly as he was walking around, trying to sell them. I saw others beating their animals. I really got upset when I witnessed a big watchdog on a chain that was barking at some guys as they were throwing rocks at him, so all I could hear was the dog whining between his barking.

"Another unpleasant event was a big guy on a motorbike driving next to us who accused me of taking his picture. After a heated exchange of words between my driver and the cyclist, they agreed to go to a police station to air the biker's complaints. At the nearby station, the policeman looked at the pictures on my camera and saw none of the biker. He only cautioned me against taking pictures of police.

"I left Bamako for Casablanca that afternoon on a fully loaded plane. After arrival in Casablanca, I flew to London for the night and then returned to the good old USA."

"James, it amazes me how you remember all the details of your trips, especially since you are still recovering from amnesia."

"Thank you, but that was a very memorable trip. However, your memory is much better than mine as you know all the diseases man can get and what the options are for treatments as well as knowing all the drugs and what they do and their side effects. Say, since you have never been to Buenos Aires and Iguaçu Falls, let us make a couple more quick trips there before we head back to Santiago."

"That sounds great, James, my dear."

The Buenos Aires airport is some distance from the city, and it took Deborah and James about an hour by bus to the bus terminal in the city, and then they had to take a fifteen-minute taxi ride to the Apart Hotel and Spa Congreso. After dinner that evening, James checked his e-mail at the hotel's business center. He found out that his assistant was handling the department's administrative work fine, and his graduate students were not having any problems with their research. It was the spring semester, and James did not have any teaching duties.

The next day following breakfast, the couple went out to explore the city near the hotel. They got to the main street that was four lanes divided by a broad grass strip. There was a monument at one place that looked like the Washington Monument in D.C. but not as high. They noted that Buenos Aires is a large city with a mixture of old and new buildings; some of the old ones are magnificent. On their walk, they had to safely watch for missing tiles and holes in the sidewalks. The city was clean with only a few homeless and no panhandling to speak of.

The following day, they took a bus tour of Buenos Aires and sat with four stewardesses from Emeritus Airlines. The stewardesses were very friendly, and James was telling them some funny jokes and stories, and they and Deborah were laughing a lot.

The next morning, James and Deborah got up early to catch a taxi to the domestic airport next to the city, about twenty minutes away. The Aerolineas Argentinas flight to Montevideo, Uruguay, was only thirty minutes. The first impression one has upon landing in Montevideo is the beautiful and unique airport terminal. It is new and shaped like a flying saucer. Inside, the first thing the couple saw was a McDonald's. Later, they would see that there was at least a half a dozen more in the city and a Burger King, but surprisingly no KFCs.

At the airport, there were no taxis around, so the couple had to take a regular bus to their hotel in the city. The bus was packed with people, and they had to stand near the front door. The ride was almost an hour with many stops to mainly let people off. As the bus neared the major part of the city, Deborah finally got to sit down in the front row with her small suitcase and backpack on her lap. The outer part of the city looked rundown, and the buildings needed repair. As they arrived in the city center, the kind driver told them the direction of their hotel at the last stop. They had to walk five blocks to the Lafayette hotel.

After getting settled in their room, they went down for lunch and then took a nap. Following their short nap, the couple took a walk wearing only light jackets as the weather was mild. The leaves on the trees were changing. They went from the hotel to the center of the city through a nice business district and saw many fine old buildings, some in good shape and others needing major repair. The other interesting item was that the city could have been anywhere in the United States as people dressed well and looked like Americans. The sidewalks were in better shape than in Buenos Aires, but still, there were tiles missing here and there, so one had to always keep one eye on the ground. They saw no bars, but the restaurants were serving all types of drinks, and there were only a few outside restaurants. The couple also saw lots of police, especially outside banks and the post office. Even at McDonald's, where they had a meal, there was a guard to keep nonpaying customers from going upstairs to use the toilets. A few homeless people were nearby sleeping on sidewalks. There were a few horse-drawn carriages with tourists getting tours. The couple stopped at an information booth, where James asked the kind lady a lot of questions about the city and its history and people. Some people began to line up behind him, so he stopped his questioning, and his last words were "I am not from the *New York Times*."

The nice lady said, "Welcome."

"Thank you."

James also commented to Deborah that he thought the kind lady knew English well.

The next day, Deborah and James took a four-hour city tour. The tour bus went all over the city with four stops. There were about twenty other people on the bus, and the guide told the group a lot about the city of one million. The country has a population of three million. The average wage is $400 a month, and this is causing a decrease in the younger population. Most couples are only having one child because of the low wages. Rents take most of their wages. One stop was at Independence Square, where there is a statue of Jose Artigas, who fought for independence.

After the tour and lunch, they had another long stroll, this time in another direction from the hotel, down to 18th July Avenue. The walk took them past Independent Square and onto a walking street that ended at the Rio de la Plata River. Many tourists mistake the extremely wide river for the Atlantic Ocean, but it is much farther south.

The following day was a rainy one. They had returned to

Buenos Aires, followed by flying to Iguaçu. After their arrival and checking into the St. George Hotel, James asked the front desk clerk, "We need a wakeup call."

The clerk asked James, "When?"

James replied, "Right now!"

She thanked him for the needed laugh.

James then said, "Five in the morning for room 508, or make it 5:08 a.m."

The clerk laughs again, along with Deborah.

Later, James and Deborah took a long walk around the small town.

The next morning, the couple boarded a bus to see the falls from both the Argentinian side and the Brazilian side. Then they had a nice walk to the lower falls. This area is better than the higher falls walk since one sees the whole falls instead of only the top of the falls. They loved the view and to watch the terrific amount of water cascading over the rocks. The water had a brown tan color in places and that disappeared by the time the water reached the bottom. On the trail, there were many coatis, like a raccoon. Later at the bus terminal, a big coati ran over and grabbed a lady's plastic bag of sandwiches and ran away with many of his fellow species chasing after him.

After a couple of hours walking around the falls, they went back to town for lunch and then to the airport for their flight to Santiago via Buenos Aires. On the second leg of the trip, James tells Deborah about some trips he took years ago.

"The trip started in Caracas, Venezuela, where I gave an invited seminar talk at their central university. The following day, I went on a tour to Angel Falls. The first night in a campground near the falls, my host and I slept outside in hammocks covered with mosquito nets. As you can probably guess, I got no sleep. Following a campout breakfast the next morning, we went to a remote runway, where I got in a two-seater, single-engine plane with me riding next to the pilot. The pilot flew over and next to the falls several times. It was a spectacular but a scary ride.

"The second stop on my trip was Bolivia. Upon my arrival at the La Paz airport, which is about fourteen thousand feet above sea level, I and several other passengers were having breathing problems, so we were given oxygen for about an hour. After receiving oxygen and drinking some coca tea, we were bused to the city, which is about a thousand feet lower than the airport. At the hotel that night and the next morning, I did not need any oxygen. Of course, I drank lots of coca tea at breakfast. Around noon, I started having breathing problems while eating lunch at McDonald's. To add to my lack of oxygen, everyone at McDonald's and in the nearby stores and streets got teargassed because the police were breaking up demonstrations of an illegal march of striking workers. Otherwise, it was a great trip seeing some beautiful mountains.

"My third short stop was in Iquitos, Peru, where I had a wonderful time riding the rickshaw motor taxis around town and cruising the Amazon in boats. This is said to be near the headwaters of the Amazon, where the Tigre and Ucayali rivers meet. The other interesting event was at a restaurant where I met an expat who spent ten years in Libya and twenty-five years in Peru as a petroleum engineer for Mobil. He now runs the bar and restaurant called the Yellow Rose of Texas, where I ate. He reminded me of Rick in the movie *Casablanca*."

Deborah asks, "What is an expat?"

"It is an American who becomes a citizen of another country."

Following their arrival in Santiago, Deborah gives James many thanks for taking her to the neighboring countries. "It was great fun to be with you, James, and to meet your friends in Brazil and see many new things, especially Iguaçu Falls. I look forward to our next adventures together."

"You are very welcome, and I look forward to more trips with you."

The couple had a long loving goodbye before they went to their respective gates for their travels to Atlanta and Puerto Williams. They agreed to meet again as soon as possible.

Chapter 5
Sightseeing in the United States

I

Following James's return from South America, he gets a call from Kim, who asks him to meet with her in the Pendleton Town Square the next day at their usual restaurant. At lunch, sitting at a booth in a quiet corner of the restaurant, Kim says, "Please give me a detailed account after we order our lunch. Someday I would like to take the trip, so if you do not object, I want to tape-record your story so I will not have to take notes."

After ordering lunch, James says, "Well, Kim, if you really want all the details of my last trip, I will begin by saying that my Chilean friend and I had a great time seeing some of Argentina, Brazil, and Uruguay. My talk at the Brazilian Nuclear Research Center was well received."

"Wait, James, our lunch is here. Let us eat, and then you can continue with your detailed narrative."

Following lunch, James says, "Again, Kim, I hope I am not getting too detailed about the account of my trips and the people I meet."

"No, please continue as I find it very interesting, and it still amazes me how you can remember all these details."

"Well, Kim, I do keep a diary, and I reviewed it before our meeting today. Maybe in the future you may want me to make a copy of my diary for you."

After James gives Kim his assurances that Brazil is not involved in a nuclear weapon program, he tells her in detail about his and Deborah's travels. Following their lunch, she thanks him for his excellent report.

Before going their separate ways, James tells Kim that he plans on inviting Deborah to the United States to see some of his favorite places in Georgia, South Carolina, and Colorado. He also informs her that he might be making a trip to Europe and Russia soon and will give a report to her following that trip.

II

James exchanges several e-mails with Deborah, and in the last one, he asks her if she would like to see some of America. She sends James an affirmative response and starts planning the trip to the United States.

After Deborah's early morning arrival in Atlanta a week later, James is there to meet her. On their way to the airport train station, Deborah says, "I had a nice long nap on the plane and also read a lot of nice things about Atlanta and Georgia."

"Well, before going onto Pendleton in a couple of days, I have planned for us to have a short visit to the city today and tomorrow take a short flight to Provincials, Turks and Caicos. I have joined the Traveler's Century Club, just like your friend Coni, and the islands are on the club list of countries and territories. I want to check off on the list at least 300 of the 327 so I can achieve platinum status in the club. Now I am a gold member, having visited more than 250 countries and territories on the club list."

"Maybe I should also join the club, and perhaps in the future, I can attend some of the dinners of the Chilean chapter that Coni attends once every couple of months."

After taking the train from the airport to Downtown Atlanta, the couple first visits the world-famous zoo. After a short walk around the zoo, with tears in her eyes, Deborah says, "James, I feel so sorry that some of the animals are in such small cages."

"Yes, I agree. As I mentioned to you before that when we go to

Colorado, I will take you to the Wildlife Animal Sanctuary, where they have rescued many animals that had lived in small cages in circuses and zoos, mainly in South America. Now the animals can roam over acres of land."

Following a long walk around Downtown Atlanta, which included going through the Coca-Cola museum and seeing the world's largest aquarium, they return to the airport and spend the night at a nearby hotel.

At noon the next day, they take a US Airways flight to Providenciales on one of the Turks Islands. On the trip, James asks Deborah, "Since we are near Cuba, would you like to read about a trip to Cuba I took many years ago?"

"Yes, that would be nice."

"Here is one of my old diaries that has everything about the trip."

> *The trip to Cuba, sponsored by Global Exchange, started after my arrival at the Ft. Lauderdale airport. There, I met several of our nine group members. After a short wait, we boarded our JetBlue flight to Havana that was a little more than an hour. Following immigration and customs, we met our host, Eliseo, and the rest of the group. The group members are:*
>
> *Marlene is from Indiana and a retired nurse.*
>
> *Carolyn was a realtor in California and now does volunteer work in the national parks.*
>
> *Anne is from New York and had just retired from nursing. She had been to Cuba three other times.*
>
> *Gigi and Chris are from California.*
>
> *Pat is also from California and works in real estate. She was the youngest lady of the group, whereas all the others are elderly.*
>
> *Vivienne is a retired professor from San Diego State University.*

Adin is the son of Vivienne and works for Boeing in Seattle.

We also had a local representative of Global Exchange, Leslie, with us periodically. She works in Cuba nine months of the year and goes to her home near San Francisco for the rest of the year. She told us that her home in California is a Yurt, a Mongolian-style tent home. We got to visit her apartment in the Milimar area.

After everyone boarded the bus with Jose, our driver drove us to the first stop that was a panoramic visit to the historic Plaza de la Revolution in Downtown Havana. The center of the city is nice with many beautiful buildings as well as some in need of restoration. The fortress is across the bay on a hill. Following lunch at the Friendship House, we visited the Literacy Museum to learn about education in Cuba, which appeared to be world class.

After the two-hour educational program, we went to the Copacabana Hotel for check-in. The hotel is in the exclusive Milimar area on the west side of Havana, about a twenty-minute ride from Central Havana. It has two hundred rooms and was built in 1980. There are two wings, each with three floors, on both sides of two main five-story buildings housing a restaurant, bar, lobby, gift shop, and business center on the ground floors. In the back is a large swimming pool next to the ocean. The east wing has a pizzeria, workout room, and massage spa. My room was on the third floor of the west wing with a deck overlooking the ocean. The room has two single beds. The bad thing (or good thing?) is that I had to walk up two flights of stairs. The hotel is in the need of repair.

After breakfast the next day, we went into Old

Havana for a tour with Eliseo. He showed the group the main attractions in the city that included a studious walk through the Casa Africa, a museum of African art. Next, we went to the nearby Muraleando community project, where there are a variety of beautifully painted walls of various people and things. We had lunch there. Following our return to the hotel in the early afternoon, the group had some free time. I chose to have a massage in the spa and later dinner in the hotel pizzeria. Afterward, I watched a beautiful sunset over the ocean from the deck.On Sunday, we went into Old Havana for a visit to the fine arts museum to see the Cuban collection, but it was closed. We then walked across the street to the Museum of the Revolution and spent some time there strolling through the building containing lots of pictures of the revolution. Outside were some airplanes and tanks used in the conflict. Next, we had a visit to central park to see La Esquina Caliente, a gathering place in the park used by Cuban baseball fans to discuss baseball (the game is extremely popular in Cuba). Instead of baseball, all we heard were the people discussing the good and bad things about U.S. politics. The enjoyable thing to see was all the fifties American cars parked and driving around the area.

Following lunch at La Moneda Cubana, we had a meeting with filmmaker Gloria Rolando to discuss race and gender in Cuba. After arriving back at the hotel, I went to a nearby grocery store that was very crowded with shoppers stocking up for New Year's parties. That evening, Marlene, Anne, and I went to a nearby restaurant, Al Pescatore, for a wonderful Italian dinner.

Following a nice buffet breakfast at the hotel

on the last day of the year, we had an early visit to Alamar Urban Garden. There, we had an educational tour of the large farm where only organic gardening is practiced. Our guide, the farmer in charge of the place, explained the medical use of some of the rarer plants. It was interesting. We had great lunch at Bodega Las Brisas in the small seaside fishing village of Cojimar that was the setting for Hemingway's Old Man and the Sea. *Following a walk in the village, we returned to the hotel to get ready to participate in a New Year's party at the hotel.*

The party took place in the hotel restaurant, bar, and lobby. That evening, following a wonderful buffet dinner, a band was playing lots of wonderful Cuban music, and folks were dancing in the bar area in front of the band.

Following breakfast and checkout of the hotel the next day, we boarded the bus for Varadero with a stop at the long Bacunayagua Bridge, built in 1959, to enjoy the scenery. In leaving Havana, the bus had to go through a tunnel under the bay. It was rated the finest architectural achievement in the country, followed by the bridge. The four-lane highway, paralleling the Atlantic Ocean most of the way, took us east about eighty miles through beautiful tree and shrub-covered hills. We passed several beautiful beaches and many farms and cattle ranches with cattle grazing in the valleys. There are a lot of oil wells in the area being worked in partnership with a Canadian company. The oil is high in sulfur, so it cannot be refined; thus, it is used in power plants for electricity generation.

We arrived in Varadero midafternoon and checked into the big and modern Melia Marina for an all-inclusive dinner and breakfast. Next to the hotel are many shops and a marina where numerous boats are anchored. Nearby is the only eighteen-hole golf course in Cuba (there is a nine-hole course in Havana), a beautiful long sandy beach and about sixty other resort hotels. It is a very exclusive area that attracts many tourists year-round.

The next morning, we departed for Cienfuegos by way of Playa Larga with a short stop at Cienega de Zapata National Park to learn of the protected area there. The park is home to two kinds of crocodiles. On our travels, we were going from north to south, from the Atlantic Ocean to the Caribbean Sea. We had lunch at Cueva de los Peces next to a deep waterflooded sinkhole, where lots of swimmers and divers were enjoying themselves. Nearby is a long sandy beach of the Caribbean Sea. We continued our drive, arriving later at the Playa Girón monument. There, we were told of the history of the area, including the nearby Bay of Pigs. We then continued traveling to Cienfuegos. Upon arrival, we visited the Palacio de Balle to view its incredible architecture and learn of its history. Later, we had a walking tour of the beautiful main plaza and theater, followed by dinner and an overnight stay at the Jaguar Hotel.

So far on the trip, it seemed like every third car we saw was an American 1950s auto, mainly Chevrolets. The reason for all the American cars was the blockade in 1960 that stopped all imports from the U.S. Cubans kept their cars and took good care of them. We wondered how they got car parts. We were told that they make their own parts, and many sedans were made into convertibles. Most of the other cars on the roads were Japanese, French, and Russian.

Eliseo was particularly good about telling

us about Cuban history, culture, and the current situation in the country. He also told us a lot about the towns that we went through. He talked about a Russian book that stipulated the amounts of staples, such as sugar, spices, and food items that every citizen should get from the government. I thought Eliseo was talking about something like Russian commandments in a book, but later, I found out it was a ration book, not a Russian book. I know I need a hearing aid.

On Thursday, we had a long drive to Camaguey, almost a two-hundred-mile trip. After our arrival and lunch, we had a bici-taxi tour of the city to see its many plazas and galleries. A bici-taxi is a bicycle with a two-seater carriage attached behind the driver. Marlene accompanied me, and it was a lot of work for the drivers pedaling their bici-taxis for the group. We stayed at the nice Gran Hotel next to a pedestrian walkway. There is an excellent view of the city from the rooftop bar. We had dinner in the evening at the hotel's Casa de la Trova restaurant with traditional music playing.

After breakfast the next morning and hotel checkout, we started for the nearby policlinic. After we boarded the bus, we had to go down a narrow street, where a jeep was parked. Jose could not get around the car, so a couple of guys nearby pushed the jeep down the street to a wider area. Our bus could then proceed on our journey, but some of us discussed what the owner would think about his car being moved. At the clinic, we received a nice tour of their facilities and attended a briefing of the clinic's services. The first thing the group had to do was to introduce themselves and tell a little of their background. When they got around to me,

I said, "My name is John, and I work in California for the Department of Energy as a scientist. In my spare time, I rob banks." Everyone had a good laugh. We learned that the clinic does the first care of treatment, and if the patent needs further help, he/she is sent to the hospital. The third level, if needed, is the patient going to a specialist. Just before the briefing ended, I asked if they have a blood bank. Everyone laughed, and then the head nurse went on to explain that indeed they do collect blood and have it in a bank.

Following our visit to Camaguey, we had a long drive to Santa Clara with a lunch stop about halfway. As we neared Santa Clara, the scenery changed from small hills and valleys to beautiful pine and palm tree-covered mountains. After reaching Santa Clara, we checked into the Canyes Hotel, had dinner, and then went to a nearby neighborhood, where we met with many members of the Committees for the Defense of the Revolution and their families. They had some food and drinks for us, and later, music was played, along with dancing in the street. I joined in and danced with several of the ladies as well as a few of the young girls. One beautiful blond girl, about ten, showed the group her ballerina routine, followed by her karate skills. It was a fun and a very memorable evening with such nice and friendly people.

The next day, we visited the mausoleum of Che Guevara. Following the tour, Eliseo dropped me and Adin at the hotel since we were not feeling well. I spent the rest of the day writing, taking a nap, and relaxing by the pool with a lot of others, including many youngers, swimming and playing ball in the pool. I was not too pleased with the resort hotel as it was some distance from the city. Me and a few others in the group would have preferred a hotel in town.

On Sunday, after bidding some of our fellow travelers goodbye at the one-gate Santa Clara airport with café and two duty-free shops, I and several others in our group boarded a JetBlue flight at 1:30 p.m., arriving in Ft. Lauderdale at three. On the flight, we flew over some beautiful blue-green waters and could see some of the Bahamas in the distance. In Ft. Lauderdale, I flew to Los Angeles via Washington D.C.

Deborah also read a little about their destination:

The group of islands next to the Turks Islands is the Caicos Islands, and both have a combined population of thirty-two thousand and are British Overseas Territories. The islands are located about 650 miles southeast of Miami in the North Atlantic Ocean. The Providenciales airport is small, and its runway is for both takeoffs and landings. It is the largest city on the islands.

After James and Deborah's arrival, they took a taxi to the Turtle Cove Hotel and checked in and had dinner at a nearby restaurant.

The next morning, the couple are on the deck of their room looking out over a beautiful marina. Debora comments, "John, the island is amazingly beautiful, and I am looking forward to seeing more of it."

"Yes, I especially like the green water washing up against the coral reefs in the bay. After breakfast, I have arranged for a driver and guide to take us on a tour of the island."

Their guide arrived midmorning and was also the driver, using his own car. Ruben is a part-time pastor and does not have a parish or church but makes house calls. He took the couple to all the major sites. James thought during the tour that there was nothing too interesting, a few classy hotels, nice houses, and several mini markets. The highlight of the tour was visiting the historic lighthouse and going to the top of Blue Mountain, which is actually a small hill. From their vantage point on the hill, they admired another beautiful green water bay that is cut off from the Atlantic Ocean by a coral reef. It was like the one they saw from their hotel room.

Ruben told the couple that there are no traffic lights on the island. He asked Deborah, "What does a green light mean?"

"Of course, it means it's okay to drive through the intersection."

Ruben then asked James, "What does a yellow light mean?"

"It means one should stop or speed through the intersection, depending on how close the car is to the intersection."

"Well, what does a red light mean?"

"It means stop."

"No, we believe that red means danger, and one should speed like hell through the red stoplight, and that is why we do not have any stoplights on the island!"

All three have a good laugh.

Near the end of the tour, Ruben informs the couple that he must make a brief stop at an elderly lady's home to give her a short sermon. "I already mentioned to you that I do not have a church or parish but make house calls. You both can join us and see an example of a typical home visit."

After the three return to the hotel, the couple thanks Ruben for the interesting tour. After a short walk to find a restaurant, they have lunch. Following their meal, they return to the hotel, where they both have a nice long nap, followed by a walk near the hotel and then dinner.

Early the next day, they return to Atlanta and get James's Smart car from the airport parking lot. Following a short drive around Georgia Tech's campus, they start their drive to Pendleton. About an hour later and halfway to Pendleton, the couple stops for lunch at the Château Élan. Following lunch at the hotel restaurant, they have a short walk around Château Élan, which is next to the classy hotel, admiring the beautiful large building. James tells Deborah that wine is made at the château from the acres of grapes around the area. There is also a nearby golf course. They then drive to Helen, Georgia, for a nice walk around the German village. On the way, they had a brief stop at Toccoa Falls.

About an hour later, James stops at the Clemson Research Park to show Deborah where he used to work and introduces her to several of the faculty and staff. Then he takes her over to Sunny Acres, his second home that is about a five-minute drive from the research park. "I designed and helped build the two-story home that sits on five acres of woods with great views of the Smoky Mountains from one side and Lake Hartwell from the other side. I have seen lots of birds, squirrels, and chipmunks as well a few snakes, frogs, and turtles on the property. A couple of times, I was lucky and saw deer, foxes, moles, raccoons, and a wild turkey. Let us take a short walk among the beautiful oak, pine, and spruce trees. Can you guess why I call this place Sunny Acres?"

"Of course. It is because the acreage sits on the sunny side of the property."

"You are correct, my dear doctor."

"The home and property are wonderful, especially the large decks on each side of the building. It's too bad, James, that we cannot go inside, but I will peek through the ground floor windows."

"There is one bedroom on the ground floor as well as a living room, dining room, bathroom, kitchen, and laundry room. Behind the two-car garage is a separate entrance to the stairs that go to the second floor. On that floor are two bedrooms, bathroom, kitchen, and living and dining rooms. The property was once part of the old Davis Plantation."

"You did a great job in designing the structure."

"Thank you. I am renting the home out to a visiting professor, who lives downstairs, and two students who camp out upstairs."

Next, they proceed to James's Pendleton home, where

Deborah receives a tour of the upstairs. Later, the two graduate students, who are living in the basement, bring up several dishes of food for a pleasant dinner. During the meal, the students ask Deborah about her home and career. After a short story of her life, Deborah asks the students where they are from and where they received their undergraduate degrees.

Mina spoke up first. "I am from Porto, Portugal, and graduated from the University of Porto."

Deborah states, "I know a lot of Portuguese, so maybe later I can practice it with you."

Diane says she grew up in Los Angeles and graduated from the University of Southern California.

After dinner, the girls return to the basement, and James shows Deborah the two guest bedrooms. "You have a choice of which room you would like to stay in."

With a smile on her face, she says, "I would rather sleep in your room on one of the twin beds and enjoy your Jacuzzi before night night."

"That would be great. Let me clean up the kitchen and do the dishes. Then I will join you for a needed good night's sleep."

Over breakfast the next morning, James tells Deborah that he had an attempt on his life last night.

"No! What happened?"

"Well, I was in my car at a stoplight in Clemson, and a car pulled up alongside of me. I turned to look at the driver, and it was the same person I saw driving away from the chemistry building during the fire in my laboratory. Then the guy threw a Molotov cocktail through the open passenger window and sped away. Then I woke from a terrible nightmare."

"James, you had me scared to death for a minute. It sounds like a terrible thing to experience during sleep."

"I usually have at least one dream at night but rarely nightmares like this one. Perhaps it is a warning about trouble in the future. Would like to see my office and laboratory this morning?"

"Of course, but let me clean up the kitchen first."

Following a nice tour of the chemistry building and introductions with his students and a few faculty members, James takes her on a drive around campus and Clemson and then back to Pendleton, where they have a walk around Pendleton Old Town Square and lunch at the Mexican restaurant.

After their meal, James tells Deborah, "I need to go to my office and catch up on some paperwork as well as check in with the dean. Would you like to stroll around Pendleton and visit the many antique shops or go back to 102?"

"It would be interesting to look at merchandise in some of the shops. I can easily find my way back to your lovely home since it is only a few blocks away. I guess you call your home 102 because that is the part of the address. It is also clever that you call the lovely pond behind 102 Golden Pond since the vegetation in the water gives it a golden look. However, before you leave, I need to borrow your house key."

"Of course. Here is my key. After my return later, we can go and have a key made for you. Then I will show you the Pendleton Library and two old plantation farms that are historic sites near here. After that, and if you wish, we can take a stroll around the South Carolina Botanical Gardens that are next to the university campus."

James gives her a hug before he departs.

After the events of the day and over dinner, James suggests an agenda for the next two days. "Tomorrow I would like to take you to Whitewater Falls that is about an hour drive from here. It is located just over the state line in North Carolina. The falls remind me of Victoria Falls in Africa but are much smaller, of course. If you are up to it, we can walk down many steps to the bottom of the falls."

"James, that sounds great, and I am sure I can handle the walk."

"After seeing the lovely falls, we can drive through the small tourist towns of Cashiers and Highlands to Walhalla for a walk about the interesting city with some beautiful buildings. Then lunch followed by returning to Pendleton via Seneca and Clemson."

"Okay, remember, I am in your hands to see your favorite places."

"The day after tomorrow, we can take a long drive through the Great Smoky Mountains National Park that is in North Carolina and Tennessee, followed by having short visits to some small historic towns on the way back here."

At the end of the weekend of their travels, James surprises Deborah by telling her that he has airline tickets for a short visit to Colorado to see his children and show her some of his favorite places. Of course, she agrees and says, "James, are you sure you can spare the time away from the university?"

"It is summer break, and most of the faculty are out vacationing as well as some of my students. The ones that are remaining have their research under way, and if they have any questions, we communicate via e-mail. I also gave the dean notice that I will retire at the end of summer since I am near retirement age."

"Wow, are you sure you want to start another new life?"

"Well, I am ready to travel more and have no more responsibility of managing the department, teaching courses, and supervising graduate students. I also want to write more, especially about my travels. Before my wonderful year with you in Chile, I had started writing a chemistry textbook that I would like to finish. I will be okay financially since I will have retirement checks from the university and Rocky Flats, my IRAs, and money from selling both of my South Carolina homes and, later, Social Security. I plan to move to Pine Shadows in Nederland, which is about a half-hour drive from Boulder. I have not told you about my mountain retreat, but I will take you there when we are in Colorado. Of course, then I will be close to my grown children."

"It sounds like you have thought out your plans well. I hope you include visiting me often."

"Of course, and I hope you will be able to accompany me on some of my visits to places I have never been to before."

After flying to Denver from Atlanta, James's three grown children are waiting for the couple at the airport reception area. Following the happy reunion and introductions of Deborah, Eric gets his car from the parking lot and picks up everyone for the ride back to his home in Boulder, where the couple will stay for several days.

That evening, over a wonderful dinner that Eric's wife had prepared, there is a discussion of everyone's activities since the young adults came to Pendleton for Ying's memorial. James asks Deborah to tell the group about her life. Next, Eric explains about his job working for a biotech company in nearby Longmont and how he and Sylvia met. "My wonderful wife works at the same company I do, and we met at CU. We bought this house last year after we were secretly married. Sorry you all were not invited to the ceremony, but it was only us, a preacher, and two of our mutual friends. We know the house is small with only two bedrooms, but housing is expensive in Boulder, and this is all we could afford. I do plan on finishing the basement sometime in the future. Before the home purchase, we were living in separate condos and before that in dorm rooms at the University of Colorado, finishing our doctorate degrees in biochemistry."

James tells Deborah, "Because of their secret wedding, I had to find out about it in an e-mail from Eric. Of course, I sent them a congratulations card with a generous check. Eric is named after my Dad's youngest brother who lives in California with his wife and two boys."

Amy speaks up, "I only have a high school degree, but a very wonderful husband. We both work in Denver for an accounting firm."

Lorrie states that she is a senior and planning to go to graduate school majoring in organic chemistry. "I am not sure if I will continue at CU or go to another university. As you can guess, our father was a big influence on our studies. I stay in a student dorm."

The next day after breakfast, James and Deborah drop Eric and Sylvia at work and borrow their car for visits to the colorful tourist town of Estes Park, Rocky Mountain National Park, and Nederland, an old mining town. On their way back to Boulder via Clear Creek Canyon, they have quick stops in Black Hawk and Central City, old mining towns that now have lots of new hotels with casinos.

Following their return to Boulder, Deborah thanks James for the wonderful day. "I especially liked the park and seeing so many deer and mountain sheep. I had hoped we would see a bear and/or a mountain lion. I was surprised by the small herd of elk in Estes Park, and the lunch we had in the restaurant of the Stanley Hotel was exceptionally good. I did see that the hotel was the same one in the movie *The Shining*."

"Well, there have been several bear visits to Estes Park, Nederland, and even Boulder looking for food, mainly in trash cans."

"I also know why you call your weekend home in Nederland Pine Shadows. It is because the home is on the shady side of the acreage and covered by shadows from the many pine trees behind the house."

"As you saw, it is much like Sunny Acres except it has a larger kitchen and a basement that houses a two-car garage, laundry room, and workshop. I like the decks with stairs on the front of the home on both the main and second floors that give one access to both floors from the driveway. Of course, the other entrances are on the enclosed stairway behind the house, where there is access from the garage to both upper levels. I am also happy that the five-acre property is next to Jefferson Country open space with a walking trail that goes to the other side of the mountain. I also love the views of Barker Reservoir, Eldora ski area, and some of the Rocky Mountains. I am sorry the couple that rent the house was not at home so I could have shown you the inside. Although I have a key, it would not have been right to enter without them being there. Since tomorrow is Saturday, I will take you and the kids to the Wild Animal Sanctuary in Keenesburg, north of the Denver's international airport. The sanctuary was founded forty years ago and has more than five hundred bears, lions, tigers, and wolves roaming on eight hundred acres of prairie. There is also an extension of the sanctuary that is in Southern Colorado, near the town of Springfield, that has 9,700 acres of hills of boulders and trees, a wonderful habitat for rescued wild animals. Well, it is time to pick up Eric and Sylvia from work. They had suggested we eat at a restaurant on the Pearl Street pedestrian street for dinner. By the way, Sylvia has another commitment tomorrow and will not join us to see the wild animals."

On their last full day in Colorado, the couple visits the old mining town of Breckenridge for lunch. James tells Deborah that instead of mining in the nearby mines, tourism and skiing are now the main attractions. On the way back to Boulder, James tells Deborah about his many past visits there. "We had a time-share condo for the first week of each year, and I would always come to Breckenridge with Margrit and the kids to ski, ice-skate, and walk around town, looking in the many shops. We would also try to eat at different restaurants for dinner. The family and I always had breakfast at the condo and would usually have lunch at the same restaurant at the base of one of the ski lifts. Breckenridge is where Margrit and the kids learned to ski. I got my ski lessons in a gym class at the university, where we would spend the weekend at another ski area above Georgetown, the old mining town we stopped at coming here this morning."

"Breckenridge is truly a lovely town, and I also enjoyed our stop on Kenosha Pass as well as going through historic South Park City in Fairplay."

On their flight back to Atlanta, James tells Deborah, "I am sorry we did not have time to visit my favorite national park, Yellowstone. It is the first national park in the U.S., established in 1872. We would have had to fly to Jackson, Wyoming, and rent a car for the drive. On my previous visits to Yellowstone, I always made a round trip of the adventure, first driving north from Jackson and going by Grand Teton National Park and then by the beautiful mountains around the park. I always stayed at the Yellowstone Lodge next to Old Faithful Geyser. After my stay at the lodge, I drove through West Yellowstone to Idaho Falls to see friends then back to Jackson. Can you guess what my favorite number 2 and number 3 national parks are?"

"I give up, dear. There are so many parks in your country. One park I would guess is the Grand Canyon."

"Correct. That is my third favorite national park. Number 2 is Yosemite National Park in California."

III

A month following Deborah's visit to the United States, James receives an e-mail from his Russian friend Misha. He is the chairman of an upcoming International Chemical Congress that the Russian Academy of Science is hosting at the Rossiya Hotel in Moscow. In the e-mail, he formally invites James to attend the congress and deliver the plenary lecture. James knew he would probably be invited as Misha had mentioned it in a previous e-mail. James accepts the flattering invitation, where all expenses will be covered by the academy. After James sent his replay, he wrote to Deborah that he will attend the conference and asks her to accompany him. Of course, they had been exchanging e-mails since Deborah's visit to the United States. Deborah excitedly accepts James's offer and starts making travel arrangements to meet him in Atlanta. A month later, they meet at the Atlanta airport and fly to Vienna.

On the long flight, Deborah asks James, "How do you like retirement?"

"Well, so far, it is okay, but we shall see."

James asks Deborah to come with him to the rear of the Boeing 777 Dreamliner, where there is no one present. In the galley, he gets on his knees, holding Deborah's hand, and says,

"Deborah, you know how much I love you, and I know you love me. Will you marry me?"

"Oh, James, I'm so happy to hear your words. I do love you very, very much, and of course, I will marry you. This is the happiest day of my life to have you ask me to be your wife. I will always love you and will not let you down."

"I have arranged for one of the stewardesses to bring the captain back and marry us. He has agreed to do this, even though it may not be legal. I wrote the usual marriage vows that are said at most weddings on a piece of paper for him. I will get the stewardess now and ask her to bring the captain back. Of course, after we arrive in Vienna, my friends have arranged a wedding ceremony for us to have a legal marriage presided over by a judge. I got this idea from the movie *Casablanca*, where Rick wants to marry Ilsa on a train by the engineer. Well, here is the captain to marry us."

After the short ceremony, the happy couple returns to their seats. James tells Deborah about some of his proposed travel plans for them in Europe. "After we arrive in Vienna in the morning and drop our luggage at the Hotel Wandl, I will take you to a friend's home. He has kindly arranged for us to legally get married in his home by a judge. Following the marriage ceremony, our hosts and a few other friends from the IAEA will have a brunch with wedding cake for us. After the party, I will show you some of the must-see things in Vienna's first district. In the evening, after a dinner of Wienerschnitzel and salad at Figlmullers, we can check into the hotel and begin our wedding night. I will tell you my other suggested travels plans after our arrival in Vienna. Now let us try to get some sleep, my dear lovely wife."

Chapter 6
Travels around Europe

I

On their second day in Vienna, James tells Deborah over a late breakfast about his tentative plans for their stay in Europe. "Today I will take you to see more of the sites in Vienna's first district. Tomorrow I will show you the places I have lived in the past followed by a visit to the Vienna International Center, abbreviated VIC, to have a late lunch with Jan, whom you met at the wedding. Jan is the section head at the IAEA of a group assisting Africa. In the afternoon, we can take the underground to Schönbrunn Palace. If you agree, we can spend our last day taking a day trip to Bratislava. The train ride only takes an hour, and I would like you to meet one of my best friends, who is a retired university professor. We are writing a book about radioactivity and nuclear energy. Following our last morning at the Wandl, we will start our honeymoon train travels in a first-class sleeper car to Istanbul, Turkey, with day visits to Budapest and Bucharest on the way. Then fly to Moscow from Istanbul.

"After the Moscow visit and my attendance at the conference, we will fly back to Vienna. After a couple of nights at the Wandl, we will travel by train for one-day visits to Salzburg and Innsbruck and return to Vienna a different way via Graz. After one-night stays in Graz and Vienna, we will take the train to Prague and stay there for several nights then to Warsaw. We may stop in Gdansk, Poland, if we have time before our return to Vienna for our flight back to the U.S."

"That sounds like a trip of a lifetime, and I am looking forward to seeing some of Europe and Russia."

"In case we do not get to visit Gdansk, you can read my diary tonight about my trip there several years ago. But first, let us start our walking tour by visiting St. Peter's Church in front of the hotel."

After their short visit to admire the beautiful inside of the church, they start their walk on the nearby Graben pedestrian street to Stephansdom Cathedral. Following a short time admiring the beautiful inside of the church, James asks Deborah if she would like to climb 343 steps to the south tower.

"Of course, my dear, as long as you accompany me."

After leaving the church, they walk down the long Karntner Strasse pedestrian street, past many shops selling everything from clothes to souvenirs, to the opera house. After James takes a few more pictures, they board a horse carriage for a ride around Vienna's ring street, past Parliament, Burggarten, Hofburg, museum, Rathaus, and Burgtheater. After continuing the journey around the inner city, they return to Stephansdom, where they leave the carriage and take a short walk to Venicea, James's favorite Italian restaurant. Over a late lunch of pizza, they discuss the morning's activities.

"James, I especially liked seeing the inside of Stephansdom, but I do not think I will climb the stairs on our next visit."

"Yes, the stair climb was challenging. I love the architecture of the old buildings in the city, and Parliament is my favorite. What you will see at VIC tomorrow will be several modern high-rise buildings. We will travel there by underground train that goes over the Danube River before reaching the UN buildings. After our lunch, Jan will take us around the IAEA building, where I worked for three years. There are other UN agencies located in attached buildings. I always finish my visit with Jan over coffee in the VIC's bar. From there, we can tell our goodbyes to Jan and go up the Vienna Tower that is nearby for a unique view of the city.

"I have a funny story about the tower. A few days after my family arrived in Vienna, I took them to the restaurant in the top of the tower. My German was not too good at that time despite taking a semester of it at the university. I ordered hot dogs and drinks for everyone in my best German. Later, the waitress brought our drinks and hot dogs, and several minutes later, she brought another round of hot dogs. When the third round arrived, I told her that we only wanted one order of hot dogs. Margrit and the kids had a good laugh."

After finishing their meal, Deborah asks James, "What will we see this afternoon?"

"Well, if you are not too tired, we can first take the underground to Belvedere Palace with its beautifully landscaped garden and great views of the rooftops of the city. After our walk around the gardens, we can have a return walk to the nearby city center and visit Karl's Church. After visiting the beautiful church, we can continue our walk past the first McDonald's in the city and a hotel that was once the headquarters of the IAEA before they moved to the VIC. We can then take a streetcar to Grinzing for a short walk and then go to Neustift an der Walde to see the house my family and I lived in for three years. If you wish, we can have dinner in a Horigan. My favorite place is Hubers that has a wonderful buffet, and we can eat in their garden."

After dinner, they return to the hotel. While James is taking a long hot bath, Deborah gets one of James's diaries and starts reading about his trip to Gdansk.

After spending three days in Prague, I flew to Gdansk, Poland, via Copenhagen, arriving early in the evening. On the plane ride from Copenhagen, a friendly lady was sitting next to me. It turned out she was a medical doctor who worked in Birmingham, England, a few days each month reviewing insurance claims for people who had been hurt in a car accident. Joanna spoke excellent English and laughed at all my jokes. She was nice, even ordering a taxi at the airport to take me to the Arkon Park Hotel, a Best Western Plus Hotel. The unfortunate thing was that the hotel was about a twenty-minute taxi ride from Old Town, where I would spend most of my two days in Gdansk.

The first evening, there were a couple of tourist groups at the hotel, and they had filled up the restaurant. Thus, I ate at the bar. The young waitress was nice and told me that she wants to work a year, save her money, and then travel a year. I also spoke with a couple from Maryland and a lady from Canada.

On Monday, it was shirt-sleeve weather and blue skies. I took about a fifteen-minute walk to a big and modern shopping center to change money. The center was three floors with a parking garage and a large variety of stores. There, I exchanged $100 for 380 zlotys. Next, I caught a taxi to old town.

I had read that Gdansk has a complicated history since it has been an important trade route and meeting point of countries, cultures, and traditions. In the early seventh century, it was a fishing village and later became a fortified city for the Polish–Lithuanian commonwealth. During the Partitions of Poland in the eighteenth century, Gdansk was incorporated into Prussia but was under German influence. On the first day of September 1939, the first shots of the Second World War occurred in Gdansk. The war destroyed 95 percent of the historic buildings in the city center. After the war, Gdansk became part of Poland and was rebuilt. In August 1980, the first regime-independent trade union was born that led to Poland's independence from the USSR.

After arrival in old town, I took a bus tour of the city. The bus started at the Golden Gate, the entrance to Old Town, and went by the World

War II Museum (that I would visit the next day), Monument to the fallen shipyard workers of 1970, Saint Bridget's magnificent church, the Grand Armory, the enormous St. Mary Church, and a large crane next to the Vistula River. In the afternoon, I boarded a tourist pirate sailing ship (the Galeon Piracki)*, that was next to a tall brown building, to go on the Vistula River from Old Town via Grudziadz, Bay of Gdansk, lighthouse, and Wistoujscie Fortress to Westerplatte (at the mouth of the river), where WWII started.*

Following the ship adventure, I had dinner on the veranda of the Hard Rock Cafe on the pedestrian walkway. There, I met a couple of young guys sitting at the adjoining table who were celebrating their graduation from the university; they were from Kurdistan and came to Poland five years ago to study. After dinner, I returned to the hotel for the night.

On Tuesday, I went back into Old Town, where I spent most of the day walking around, visiting churches as well as the war museum. In the museum were several groups of school kids of all ages. I had tears in my eyes as I viewed the many pictures of the atrocities of the two world wars.

The tour guide told me yesterday that the tourist season did not start until next month, but there were still large groups of tourists everywhere in the city. On this walk, I first went to St. Bridget's church that dates back to the fourteenth century; it was badly damaged during WWII but restored in the 1970s. St. Katherine's Church has the largest carillon in Central Europe with fifty bells; next door is the Museum of Tower Clocks with seventeen clocks on exhibit. At the entrance to Dluga (Long) Street is the Golden Gate, where a mile-long pedestrian walkway begins. At the other end is a bridge going over a canal. On the walkway are many shops, cafés, and restaurants, not to mention buskers, jugglers, magicians, and organ grinders. Other things I visited were the Fountain of Neptune, Green Gate, Long Riverfront, Main Town Hall, and St. Mary's Church, one of the largest brick churches in the world that took over 150 years to build, starting in 1343. One funny thing I saw during my walk was a guy on a bike with an Uber food box on the rear fender.

On Wednesday, I went by taxi to the Gdansk airport to catch my flight to Frankfurt. Security was fast and easy. The airport is new and modern and has twenty gates and lots of shops and restaurants, including a McDonald's. I had lunch at The Flame restaurant, and one of the waitresses looked just like Angelina Jolie. The television news had a story about the flooding in Warsaw caused by heavy rains; the winds were so strong they blew several roofs off homes. I spent most of the time on the flight to Frankfurt talking with a young Hollywood-handsome army sergeant about his work and assignments. He had been in the army almost twenty years traveling to different bases to advise on terror attacks. He had spent a couple of years in Iraq. His mother is American Indian.

In Frankfurt, I spent the night at the Park Inn hotel again. The next morning, I left for Denver at eleven and played chess and watched a Clint Eastwood movie on the flight. I took a Super Shuttle home after the plane landed in Denver.

After breakfast the next morning, James starts the conversation with Deborah by recalling their wonderful buffet breakfast. "I especially liked the yellow cheese paste to spread on the whole wheat rolls."

"I agree. There was lots of good food to choose from, and I was surprised they have champagne available."

"I was also surprised at the large number of tourists in the city, more than I have ever seen. Are you up for a long day in the city?"

"Of course. I can hardly wait to ride the famous giant Ferris wheel at the Prater and see where you worked and, of course, to visit Schöenbrunn Palace with its glamorous rooms and have a long walk in the gardens. From what I read, we could spend a whole day there, including trying to get out of the high shrub maze."

Following their day's activities at the Prater, VIC, and the palace, they have early dinner, followed by their return to the hotel to prepare for the visit to Bratislava the next morning.

II

The early train ride to Bratislava, the capital of Slovakia that sits next to the banks of the Danube River, took only an hour, passing through woods and farmland and finally on a long bridge connecting the two countries before reaching the train station. Following their arrival in Bratislava, James took Deborah on a walking tour of Old Town on the cobbled streets, with several fountain-filled piazzas and connecting a warren of medieval cobbled alleyways. There are many pastel-colored, red-roofed townhouses surrounding the streets. Numerous clothing stores and souvenir shops are on the ground floors of the beautiful buildings as well as restaurants and bars. The notable buildings in Old Town are the Gothic St. Martin's Cathedral, Grassalkovich Palace, Primate's Palace, Slovak National Theater, and several museums housing collections of artwork, Jewish history, music, and weapons. Bratislava Castle sits on a hill and is visible from most parts of the city as well as from the other side of the Danube; it was once the residence of the Habsburg dynasty that ruled over much of Europe for centuries.

James and Deborah met Tibor in a classy restaurant in Old Town, and after a long lunch, they went to Tibor's university for a tour, followed by James giving a seminar talk to some of the faculty and students. Deborah told James later that she enjoyed his presentation, especially the pictures. Before going to the train station, Tibor took the Czermaks to the Pharmaceutical Museum, which contains 2,500 fascinating artifacts dating back to the fourteenth century. When the Czermaks said their goodbyes to Tibor, Deborah told him that seeing the museum was a great way to finish their wonderful visit to a lovely city.

Following their return to Vienna by train and dinner, they went to the opera house to hear the Vienna Philharmonic Orchestra play. After the opera, they returned to the Wandl to pack for their early morning train ride to Budapest.

III

After their train ride in a first-class car and storing their luggage in a locker at the train station, the Czermaks took a taxi to the city center. James was reminded that it is always a joy to visit Budapest. Formerly part of the Austro-Hungarian Empire, James thinks it is the world's second most beautiful city with Prague being in first place. The Hungarian capital, once composed of the separate towns of Buda, Obuda and Pest, were officially unified in 1873 and named Budapest. The city lies on both banks of the Danube. Many historic churches and beautiful old houses cover its steep wooded hills. The Royal Palace stands proudly on a hill overlooking the city center.

Deborah and James first went to the city park to see Budapest's Szechenyi Baths; Budapest is known as the city of spas for its 120 geothermal springs. They had a look inside of

St. Stephan's Basilica and then had a walk up to the viewing platform to have a 360-degree view of the city. They continued to wander around the city, seeing more of the remarkable sites, and rode the Metro.

To their surprise, mysteriously and seemingly out-of-nowhere vendors, notably Russian and mostly old women, would unfurl from their bags, their coats, or whatever an array of beautiful hand-worked items. When James captured this on film, the items and vendors quickly and mysteriously disappeared. Later in the afternoon, they went to the plush Casino Schönbrunn, a beautiful yacht on the Danube. Deborah did a bit of gambling, including her first try at Roulette, and was happy that she won more money than she spent. James enjoyed her excitement.

For dinner, James suggested that they eat at the Pragai Vencel restaurant near Parliament House with an outdoor table next to the Danube. James told Deborah it was the restaurant he and Margrit had eaten at for all their dinners on their trip to the city years ago. The Hungarian dish *Hortoba'gy palacsinta* that they both ate was delicious. James also told his charming wife how to say cheers in Hungarian, which is *egészségére*. He told her to be careful, that if she mispronounces it, she is saying something obscene.

Over dinner, they discussed the many remarkable sites they had visited or walked by on their short visit to the city. Deborah commented, "I especially liked how the luscious Danube splits the city down the middle with Pest on one side and the hilly and historic Buda on the other side, with several museums and very plush parks. What stands out is Buda Castle that crowns Castle Hill and contains three remarkable museums. Nearby is also Matthias Church, an important landmark on the hill."

"Of course, I liked the Pest side of the river the best, with my favorite being Parliament House with its three-hundred-foot dome, gargoyles, and neo-Gothic spires. It was great that we were able to tour the building. The architecture of some of the older buildings is remarkable."

IV

Later that evening, they go to the train station, obtain their luggage, and board the train for an overnight nine-hour ride to Bucharest. The Czermaks got little sleep that night, even though they were in a first-class sleeper cabin. After their arrival, they stored their luggage at the station and took a taxi to the city center in search of a nice-looking restaurant for a late breakfast. Over their meal, James tells Deborah about the recommended tourist sites that are the best places to visit. "This guide starts out by stating that Romania's capital is rich with a storied history and was once known as Little Paris for its elegant architecture. The guide highly recommends a stroll down Calea Victoriei, where one can see the country's monuments and grandest buildings. There are other charming cobbled streets that weave through the Old Town and are lined with bookshops, cafés, restaurants, and theaters. Nearby are city parks and museums. The map in this booklet should help us find these interesting places.

"The guide also recommends visiting Curtea Veche, an open-air museum, and the National Museum of Romanian History. The top attraction is the Palace of the Parliament that has three thousand rooms. It used to be called the People's House by the dictator Nicolae Ceausescu, who used it as his family's residence and as a seat of government. Now a small portion of the building houses Romania's parliamentary headquarters and the National Museum of Contemporary Art.

"On my short visit here years ago, I remember getting lost in this enormous building. The other thing that stands out in my mind is getting called into the American Embassy since I was taking pictures outside the embassy. The security person wanted to see if I was taking pictures of the embassy with my video camera, which I was not. I know never to take pictures of embassies, police stations, and military installations."

"James, it sounds like we will be spending a good part of the day in parliament!"

"Yes, indeed. The tourist guide also advises to see the Romanian Athenaeum that is home to the George Enescu Philharmonic Orchestra and resembles an ancient Greek temple with a peristyle of six ionic columns and a 120-foot-high dome. Other must-see places are Stavropoleos Church, the Old Princely Court, Church and Museum, Revolution Square, and the Arch of Triumph. Remember, we did see the arch on the taxi ride."

"Yes, the arch is very impressive. It was interesting what the taxi driver, who spoke a little English, told us about the arch being dedicated to the Romanian soldiers who fought in the First World War, and it continues today to serve as the central point for military parades."

"Shall we finish our meal with a little more food so we can skip lunch and see more of this interesting city? Deb, are you ready for a lot of walking?"

"Of course, but first, please order me a piece of apple pie."

Following a long, wonderful day seeing the major sites in the city, James and Deborah are now in the restaurant car of their train to Istanbul. James starts the conversation after they finish dinner. "Do you agree that it was a wonderful day in such a fascinating city with so much to see?"

"Yes, I agree. I wish we could have spent more time in the National Museum of Romanian History and its collections of religious and royal treasures. The open-air museum built on the site of the Old Princely Court was also worth seeing. It was interesting to hear that the Curtea Veche was once the home of Vlad the Impaler, who inspired Bram Stoker's tale of Dracula."

"Although I have been there before, I saw some new things at the awesome Palace of the Parliament. I also enjoyed seeing for the first time Stavropoleos Church and to read that it was built in 1724 by a Greek monk, Ioanikie Stratonikeas. The Orthodox church features fine stone and wood carvings and is surrounded by a wonderful garden courtyard filled with eighteenth-century tombstones."

"James, I am ready for bedtime. Let us make our way back to our sleeper car."

V

The train ride from Bucharest ended early morning in Istanbul. This time the Czermaks slept much better than the ride the night before. They obtained their Turkish visas at the train station and then went to their hotel in the center of the fascinating city with many beautiful mosques. After storing their luggage at the hotel, James arranged an all-day tour. At nine, a van with driver, guide, and four other tourists arrived at the hotel to pick up the Czermaks. The guide first tells the group that they will see the most popular landmarks of the one-time Ottoman capital. At the Grand Bazaar, they will watch a handicraft demonstration and see the Hippodrome, where hundreds of spectators are gathered and marvel at centuries-old attractions in the Topkapi Palace and Hagia Sophia Museum. The tour also includes a multicourse Turkish lunch.

The tour began with a visit to one of the Eight Wonders of the World, the Hagia Sophia Museum that occupies a unique place in architecture history; James especially liked this stop since he considers himself to be a part-time architect. The tour continued with a drive by the Blue Mosque. The guide explained that it is the only imperial mosque in the world that was originally built with six minarets and that it takes its name from the beautiful blue tiles in the interior. At the next stop, the guide and passengers got to have fifteen minutes to view the social and sporting center of old Byzantium, the Hippodrome Square. The van then went to Kapali Carsi, which is next to the Grand Bazaar, where the group received a brief handicrafts presentation. Following the presentation, everyone got some time to wonder through the bazaar, followed by a delicious lunch.

After their meal, the group boarded the van for a short visit to the Haci Besir Aga Camii Mosque, followed by a tour of Topkapi Palace. The palace was home to Ottoman Sultans, and on the two-hour tour, the group got to see the Baghdad Kiosk, Imperial Treasury, and collections of Chinese celadon ceramics. The palace also contains a harem that only the sultan and his ladies could occupy. The tour concluded with a drive around more of the city and dropping each group member at their respective hotel. James and Deborah were the last to return to their hotel.

Before dinner, the Czermaks had a walk near their hotel, followed by having a meal at a nearby restaurant. Over their dinner, they discussed their day. "Deb, I thought it was a great tour of a beautiful and fascinating city."

"Yes, I agree. Our best stop I think was at the Blue Mosque. It's amazing how they built such wonderful buildings during those ancient times, especially the beautiful blue ceramics."

"Well, we must retire early tonight and prepare for a dawn-rising flight to Moscow."

Chapter 7
Russian Adventures

I

On the plane trip from Istanbul to Moscow, James starts the conversation. "Deb, we are now flying over the Black Sea and will soon be above the North Caucasus. I hope that we will be able to see the mountains from the plane, especially Mont Elbrus, the highest mountain in Europe. We do have blue skies. In Vienna, I received an e-mail from an old friend that had just returned from a trip to the North Caucasus. He thought I would like to read about his adventure in the e-mail attachment. I printed it out and read it the other night. Here it is, and I think you will find it a good read."

"Of course, my wonderful husband. I will start reading it now."

> Dear John, old friend,
>
> Since you are a traveling man, I thought you would find the attachment to this e-mail interesting. The attachment is a log of my recent trip to the Northern Caucasus. I based the narrative on a brochure I had received from a Spiekermann travel agent, who arranged the trip.
>
> Happy reading, Gary.

> On the first Sunday in September, I took a Turkish Airline flight from London to Adler Sochi via Istanbul (a very big and modern airport with twenty gates in each of seven terminals and many shops and restaurants, including Burger King and Wimpies), arriving at three the next morning. On the

flight, I finely won about as many games of chess as the plane's computer.

At the Sochi airport, I met our traveling group—Bruce (a lecturer, historian, and linguist from the UK), Tom (a retired dentistry professor from Canada who was born in Czechoslovakia), Ellie (a retired realtor), and Dani (a retired army captain and pharmacist, with a PhD and a great laugh and sense of humor). Olga, our local guide, was a young and lovely Russian lady. David, our driver, picked us up for a ride to the Hotel Adriano, where we spent only a few hours freshening up.

Before we left the hotel, Bruce gave a short lecture about what we will see and do on the trip. He first told us that Sochi hosted the winter Olympics in 2014; cold outdoor sports were held twenty miles from Sochi and indoor sports in the city. Bruce continued. "Sochi is within European Russia and is in the northern part of the Caucasus region between the Black Sea and Caspian Sea. Historically, North Caucasus was the land of famous warriors and strange archaic traditions, which is turning to peace now. We are lucky to explore the North Caucasus in the most beautiful time of the year, when summer turns to autumn; that is the time of weddings, red-yellow-green forests, and abundant tables."

Bruce also mentioned that our fascinating journey through the North Caucasus will touch on historical monuments, isolated settlements, towers, orthodox monasteries, majestic landscapes, and cultures that have survived centuries without outside influence: a very off-the-beaten-track journey to an area of the world that is least visited by foreigners and travelers.

Bruce continued. "The trip will start from

Abkhazia, a partially recognized country, which was the pearl of Georgia in the Soviet period, and marvel at other Northern Caucasian Autonomous republics, including Kabardino-Balkaria, Ossetia, Ingushetia, Chechnya, and several others. We will move from developed west to wild east, from subtropical and friendly Abkhazia to Dagestan, where we will explore ethnicity and the history from Stone Age to Soviet era. We should witness daily life of highlanders in the high mountains with centuries-old forests that are filled with oaks, firs, and wild blueberries. Our adventure will include the exploration of the most visually striking and culturally different villages."

After breakfast on Monday, we boarded a small bus and drove to the border between Russia and Abkhazia for a visit to Old Gagra. At the border, we had to go through an immigration and customs checkpoint. In Gagra, we walked in the park, which was established before the Russian revolution. Afterward, we continued to Achandara village, which is one of many traditional villages. We witnessed the lifestyle of one of the families, learned how to cook Abysta (Abkhazian bread), and had lunch with the family. After the family visit, we drove to Sukhumi, the capital of the Abkhazia. Upon arrival, we visited the national museum, took a walk in the historical part of the town, visited the Botanic Gardens, and had dinner at the Gastro Kub restaurant. We stayed overnight at the fancy four-star Leon Hotel.

On Tuesday morning, we drove to New Athos, a town located close to Sukhumi. Then we explored the ruins of the first capital of the Abkhazian Kingdom, New Athos cave, monastery (which was established in XIX century by monks who came from Greece), and one of the most beautiful railway stations of the Soviet era. In the evening, we drove back to Old Gagra and had dinner in a restaurant that was built in 1902. We stayed at the four-star Kontinent hotel.

The next morning, we went to the mountains to enjoy the beautiful scenery of Ritsa Lake and visit one of Stalin's dachas, which was erected near the lake. We also took a ride on Stalin's motorboat around the lake, and everyone got a chance to drive part of the way. After wine tasting and lunch in the mountains, we traveled back to cross the Russian border near Sochi. After the border crossing, we went to Central Sochi to see the most important architectural sites like old sanatoriums, the marine station, art museum, and the memorial of Russian victory in the war of 1828–1830 against Turkey. After we finished the sightseeing of Sochi, the group had dinner at the Quay of Sochi, followed by going to the railway station to get on the night train to the Central Caucasus. I did not get much sleep in my private cabin because of the train's noise and rocking.

On Thursday morning, we had breakfast on the train during the crossing of a large plain with lots of farms with cornfields, cattle, and sheep herds. At nine, we arrived at Mineralnye Vody train station. There, we were met by two new drivers with two Russian Nissans and started our adventure to Djily-su, located at the foot of Mount Elbrus, with a few thermal springs and waterfalls. There, we had a picnic-style lunch and afterward continued to Shaukam pass (8,800 feet) to reach Tyrnauz, a ghost town in the middle of nowhere, which was a miner's settlement in the Soviet era. We then continued our drive to the Terskol Mountain resort, which is 6,600 feet above sea level. The ski resort is a base for hikers who are going up to the snow-covered peak of Mont Elbrus, the highest mountain in Europe. We overnighted at the four-star Azau Star ski resort. Interestingly, there was a large poster in the hotel that showed a skier going downhill, and it was titled "Ski Colorado."

On Friday, we left the beautiful mountains and hills and drove parallel to a river on a nice asphalted four-lane road to Nalchik, the capital of Kabardino-Balkaria. Our first stop was the National Museum, where we met Felix, the master of Shashka (Adygean long swords). We enjoyed the displays at the museum and the Kabardian martial arts performance with his disciples. They showed us their martial art skills with swords and daggers. Afterwards, we enjoyed a Kabardian cuisine lunch of fish soup and pizza in the city. Following lunch, we drove to Vladikavkaz to visit the Ossetian church, Armenian Church, Sunni Mosque (built by a European designer before the revolution), and some mansions in the historical part of the city. The city is nice with tree-lined streets. Later, we participated in a cooking class and tried to cook the famous Ossetian pie. That night, we stayed at the beautiful hotel Aleksandrovsk (four stars).

After breakfast on Saturday, we explored the mountains of North Ossetia (light-jacket weather; the area gets about 325 days of sunshine, no snow, and little rain). We first visited the greatest necropolis in the Caucasus (near Dargavs village). Then we continued to Khidikus village to have our lunch at "Sunny Valley" restaurant. Ulga told us this is where she got married with over four hundred guests. Her husband is a diplomat, and she teaches English at a university. Afterward, we explored the highest monastery of Russia, which is located near

Khidikus, followed by driving back to Vladikavkaz for a relaxing walk in the downtown. Before dinner, we met and listened to "Kona," a local folk ensemble. We stayed a second night at the hotel Aleksandrovsk.

Sadly, today Ulga left us, and we got a new guide from Moscow, Vlad, as well as two new drivers. We first visited the market of Vladikavkaz, where we tried the local specialties and got food supplies for a picnic lunch. The merchants were mainly Koreans. Then we started our way toward the mountains of Ingushetia. We visited the most interesting medieval settlements with defensive towers—Erzi, Egikal, and Vovnushki—and saw the most ancient Christian church in Russia, Tkhaba-erdy. Continuing our drive, we arrived in Grozny later that afternoon. We enjoyed dinner and a panoramic view at the restaurant situated on the thirty-third floor of the Grozny Hotel. After dinner, we took a short walk around the city center to marvel at the illuminated mosque known by the locals as Heart of Chechnya. It is one of the grandest mosques in Europe. We overnighted at the wonderful five-star Grozny city hotel.

After breakfast on Monday, we took a city walking and sightseeing tour, which gave us an opportunity to explore Downtown Grozny. We stopped to see a rehearsal of the ethnic dance troop, which was very entertaining. After a short coffee break, we visited the museum of A. Kadyrov and the National Museum. Following a traditional-style lunch, we went to Kezenoyam Lake (the biggest lake in the mountains of the Caucasus) for some time on rowboats. We also visited another impressive mosque in Argun town and had dinner at the three-star Kezenoyam hotel, next to the lake, where we spent the night.

The next morning, we started our drive to experience a big change of landscapes that had a lot of impressive views on the way. Dagestan truly differs from the other Caucasus and reminded me of the huge mountains of Central Asia. First, we visited a factory specializing in the production of burkas (traditional Caucasian felt coats) and visited a mill where villagers make Urbech (traditional paste of flaxseeds and ground-up apricot pits—Dagestani Nutella). Then we continued our way to Dagestan, stopping at an Untsukul village on the way. Although wood carving has been popular nearly everywhere in Dagestan, the village of Untsukul has won special fame in this area of expertise. For two hundred years, Untsukul masters have been developing unique methods of decorating spoons, plates, and walking sticks. We explored this ancient village and its craft tradition. We ended the day attending a Muslim wedding with dinner and watching some of the attendees dancing. After the wedding, we went to Gunib village in the rain for two nights at the Eagles Nest hotel (three stars).

After breakfast on Wednesday, we went to visit Sogratl village to interact with the local people. We stopped by a school in Sogratl and learned more about the daily life of students. Next to the school is a small production factory making woolen carpets; we got to see how they were made. Then we drove to the historical area called Andalal. Here, local people in the XVIII century stopped the fifty thousand soldiers army of Nadir Shah. After a visit to the museum of battle, we had lunch in the open-air café

"Andalal." Our next stop was Chokh village to see its magnificent architecture and meet local young men who are reviving their village. We continued to Gunib, a village where Imam Shamil (the famous leader of Gazavat in the XIX century) was captured. This war lasted for twenty-nine years. In Gunib, we visited the small historical museum dedicated for the village. We spent a second night at the Eagles Nest.

We left Gunib on Thursday and drove to the Lak village, named as Balkhar. On the way, we stopped at the underground waterfall of Salta. Balkhar is famous for a very archaic ceramic technique. Afterward, we went to Kubachi, the most famous craft village of Dagestan. We were told that the jewelry of the Kubachi region is exhibited at the Metropolitan museum in New York and the Hermitage in Saint Petersburg. We had lunch with one of the jewelers, followed by exploring the life of jewelers and their village. The group stayed overnight at the guest house of Rasul Kurtaey, one star, in Kubachi after a nice dinner.

On Friday morning, we explored the daily life of people in the Kubachi village. We also had a thirty-minute hike to the top of a hill to see a deserted village. Afterward, our group headed to Derbent and made a stop for lunch in one of the most ancient towns of Russia. After our group arrived in Derbent and checked into the Scarlet Sails Hotel (three stars) for two nights, we had the afternoon free until dinner.

The group started Saturday by exploring the Old Town of Derbent with its abundance of historical UNESCO sites and ample chances of meeting local people. We visited Naryn-Kala, the citadel of

Derbent, and walked around the narrow streets of the Old Town and saw the oldest mosque of Russia dating back to the eighth century. We also got to see the old baths or "hamams." After lunch, we visited the Muslim shrine of a saint and Kyrkhlyar cemetery. This is a burial place of forty warrior-martyrs, who, according to the legend, brought Islam to Derbent. Afterward, we went to the Armenian Church that was turned into the Museum of Carpets and Rugs. The group overnighted again at the Scarlet Sails hotel next to a Caspian Sea beach.

After breakfast on Sunday, we started our way to the north and arrived in Bunaksk, the former capital of Dagestan. Upon arrival, we enjoyed a visit to the museum in the former theater, which resembles the famous Vienna opera house. We then continued our way to the deepest canyon of Russia named as Sulak to enjoy the panoramic view. Afterward, we were hosted for lunch by the owner of a fruit garden who used to work in the high-tech business. After a delicious lunch and tour of the fruit garden, we drove to Sary Kum and observed a unique sunset followed by a wonderful evening dinner in a local restaurant. We stayed at the four-star Central City hotel.

After breakfast on Monday, we visited the colorful bazaar of Makhachkala, where people from all over the country join to sell their goods. Later, we explored the city center and tried the traditional cuisine in a local restaurant. Afterward, we headed to the airport of Makhachkala to catch our UT (Russian plane) to Moscow at eight, arriving two hours later. On arrival at Moscow's Vnukovo airport, we continued our return on a Turkish airline plane to London via Istanbul.

On the flight, I recalled some of the things not mentioned above. Cattle, horses, sheep, geese, and chickens were mostly free-range animals, and periodically, they were on the sides of the roads or crossing the roads. The weather was light jacket the whole time with no rain. Moscow was cold.

"James, I find this very interesting, and I wish we had been along on Gary's trip."

"Well, if you want to read more travel stories, I have one of my trip diaries in my suitcase, and I can get it for you if want to read about my trips years ago to the 'Stan countries.'"

"Of course, but I think the stewardesses will be serving lunch soon, so get your diary after we finish lunch. I am sorry I do not have anything for you to read."

"Well, I can try and beat the airplane's computer playing chess."

After their meal, Deborah starts to read about James's travels to the Stan countries:

The morning following the conference in Moscow, where I gave a paper on my actinide separations research, I took a taxi in heavy traffic to Domodedovo, Moscow's newest airport (the same airport I flew into from London). I had plenty of time for lunch at the airport before my flight to Tashkent.

Upon landing in Tashkent, as usual, most of my fellow passengers applauded. My guide, Bakhrom, and driver, Takhangiv, picked me up at the small airport and took me to the Shodik Palace hotel. The remodeled Russian hotel was not bad but no bathtub. Bakhrom has two wives and six kids, two by one wife and four children by the other wife. He is a Muslim.

Tashkent has a population of four million and

the country thirty million of which 80 percent are Muslim. Their currency is the Shur of which about two thousand equals one U.S. dollar. One of the main industries is the manufacture of Chevrolet's Matiz, a small car.

On Thursday morning, Bakhrom picked me up at nine, and Takhanagiv's son was driving. We first went on a city tour and saw that it is a nice clean city with no graffiti and a moderate amount of traffic, very unlike Moscow. Then we took rides on two of the three underground subways.

Following the subway trips, we went to the Monument of Courage, a bronze statue of a man and woman standing on a crack in the ground, representing the people who died in the 1966 earthquake of Richter scale eight and a half and the worst the country had ever experienced. The earthquake caused 7,800 families or 300,000 people to become homeless after the tragedy. Most of these people went to other USSR countries while new apartments were built to replace their homes that had had walls made of straw and mud. Later, we went to see a couple of mosques that were very impressive.

That evening, Bakhrom and I went for a walk around a nice manmade lake. As we started our walk, a lovely young lady, who had heard us speaking, came over and asked if she could join us. She wanted to practice her English. The young lady told us that she had spent three years in Singapore learning English and now works as a secretary for the president of a company. She would like to be a tour guide. We also went around a nice outdoor shopping area, where local artists were displaying their paintings.

On Friday morning, Bakhrom and his senior wife picked me up at nine. They were in his Chevrolet, and later, she got out near their home on the other side of town. Then we continued to the beautiful mountains. After a two-hour drive, we arrived at the Chimgam ski area. It had chairlifts that we would have gone up on if we would have had time for a visit. Next, we drove down to nearby Lake Charbak. The mountain road was rough with many turns. Near the ski area and lake, there are many dachas. At the lake, there are a couple of fancy hotels and lots of swimmers and sail and speedboats in the water. The lake had a nice beach. After seeing these sites, we made our way back to the city, thus making a round trip.

We got back to the hotel for a late lunch of Greek salad, followed by a dish of ice cream. The lady at the next table had ordered in English, so I asked her where she was from. She said Iran and was there for a week's vacation. The nice-looking lady told us that she works for a public relations company (she did not want to name) in Tehran. She wants to go to Colorado to river raft on the Colorado River and has already applied for her visa.

Following lunch and an hour nap, I took a walk around the neighborhood to find that there are wide streets with many shops. I found an Internet café and sent out some e-mails. After the Internet café visit, I sat at an outdoor table of another café near the hotel. There was a movie theater next to the café, and I enjoyed watching the people going inside— from couples of girls to families with beautiful small children. At the entrance to the theater, there were three guards checking purses and backpacks. Another thing that I noticed was that all the trees had their bases painted white up about three feet from the ground. Later, the clerk at the hotel told me that it was for insect control.

That night at the hotel before dinner, I met an Australian lady from Sydney who was doing about the same thing I was doing—touring the Stan countries. She and her husband were with another couple. I was invited to join the group for dinner. Over a dinner of a Quattro Stagioni pizza, I told the foursome that I used to have a photographic memory, but now I am running out of film. They also laughed a lot when I told them that I am so germophobic that when I want some gum following a meal in a restaurant, I peel off some gum under the table but that I wash it before chewing it.

After dinner, I met an Irishman who works in Tashkent one month then goes home for another month. Then he repeats the routine. His work deals with financial help for the country.

On Saturday, Bakhrom and I took a fast train to Samar with monuments that were made in Korea. Samar has a population of about half a million and is one of the oldest cities in the country. On the roadside of the tracks were many cattle and goats; we were told that the animals go home at night. We also passed many farms and two towns.

Upon our arrival at Samar, there was a car and driver waiting for us to show us the following monuments: Imom Al Bukhovriy, Amir Temple, Registon, Bibiknonum, Shokhi Zindor, and the Mizzzo Vlugbek Observatorium. The visit was very worthwhile.

On our way back on the train, there were two small boys sitting behind us with their mother across the aisle. They had gotten a bag of potato chips from the train vendor. Later, I reached back like I was going to take the bag, and the surprised boys quickly jumped back with their bag of chips. Later, one of the darling boys handed me some chips.

Next, my travels took me to Bishkek, Kyrgyzstan, which has the roughest airport runway so far on the trip. Bishkek's Manas airport is not as nice as Tashkent's. At the airport, surprisingly, there were about twelve U.S. Air Force cargo carrier planes parked some distance from the terminal.

The first night in my hotel room, I was awoken by a bunch of young people in the next room making lots of loud noise. After a while trying to sleep, I yelled out in some mix of foreign languages, and they stopped. I did not want them to know I spoke English.

The next day, my driver drove to some of the important things in the city, such as the Ala-Archa Park and the Manas Park, both at 5,400 feet in elevation. In Bishkek, as was in Tashkent, I saw no beggars on the streets, and most of the people were nice and well-dressed.

After my short visit to Bishkek and on the way to the airport, which was quite a way from the city, I saw a variety of houses, some old, some new ones, and even some being built as well as lots of Coca-Cola signs. At the airport (as well as in Tashkent's airport), departing passengers had to take off their shoes in a second (more thorough) inspection than the preliminary one at the entrance to the airport. However, they did not inspect liquids, and later, I even took the large bottle of water with me on board the plane that I had purchased in the city. On the airport bus going to the Air Astana airplane, there was an American standing next to me from Washington. He was with his wife and another couple. We exchanged a few words about where we live and work.

On the flight, the lady behind me and next to the emergency door had two purses stored on the floor, and the guy next to her had his suitcase under my seat. Surprisingly, the flight attendants did not question this. All other flights, the passengers in the emergency row must place their belonging in the overhead storage areas. Everyone was served lunch with meat and vegetables, but we had no knives or forks.

The plane to Almaty, Kazakhstan, was half full, and the flight was only thirty-five minutes. In Almaty, I was met by my guide, Nazlral. The next day, she and our driver took me to the mountains via lots of traffic. It appeared that the people drive crazy here, changing lanes by just cutting another car off. Our driver drove me mad because he kept hitting the gas and letting up on it, jerking my head back and forth. A beautiful river followed the canyon road that we were traveling on.

We went to a mountain lake with a skating rink, and Nazlral told me that it is one of the highest in the world. There was a cable car there that went higher than the skating rink. Then we had lunch in a tent, called a Yurt, which is common in Mongolia. At lunch, there was a wide variety of food. After the meal, we went to a hill overlooking the beautiful city. There was an amusement park on the hill as well as several places to eat and buy souvenirs.

From Almaty, I took a flight back to Moscow.

"James, your visits to the Stan countries sound great, and it reads like you had a wonderful time with no problems."

"I do have wonderful guardian angels who look out for me. Go ahead and read about my next trip while I try to get a little sleep."

"Okay, here I go. Sweet dreams."

> *I am now on the plane in Moscow, getting ready to leave for Kaliningrad. The plane is full of almost all-American Baptists working all over Russia with their families. They are going to a conference in Poland (near the coast) for a week. One guy I spoke with works in former Stalingrad with his pregnant wife and three young daughters. The airport almost seemed like a preschool! So far, the plane is quiet. I think the children have fallen asleep since the plane is very warm. Adam, whom I visited with at the airport, said he has been in Russian for over two years; the first year in Moscow and now former Stalingrad. He said that they (his entire family) must leave Russia once a year to get their visas renewed. The first year, it was every six months. Another fellow with an Asian wife (from Oklahoma) and no children runs a parish in the major city south of Yekaterinburg, and he hears a lot about the contaminated lake and the Myack nuclear accident. These missionaries would make good eyes and ears for the U.S. on the pulse of the Russian people.*
>
> *I was thinking during the flight that I will hate leaving all my friendly fellow Americans at the Kaliningrad airport, especially all the cute kids. Everyone thought I was with their group and was anxious to meet me. One single gal next to me was from Arkansas and has been in the major city above Vladivostok for about ten years. She goes to Seoul, South Korea, once a year for her visa renewal. The lady across the aisle was from a small town near Asheville and really misses North Carolina. Her*

husband and three boys (seven, nine, and twelve years) were in the back of the plane. I had an aisle emergency row, but I think the legroom was tighter than the other seats, which is really the tightest I have ever flown in. When I was taken to the airport yesterday, we got off the busy Leninsky Prospect Boulevard and took some back roads through small villages. There were several housing projects with big homes being built for the wealthy. There are two terminals at the Sheremetyevo airport—it is the airport I used to fly in and out of during the late seventies to early eighties.

In Kaliningrad, I had an elderly lady, Katarina, as a guide, with a young driver, and they first took me to one of the outer old fortresses surrounding part of Kaliningrad. Then we went to the cathedral in town, followed by a visit to the technical university and the Institute of Oceanography, where the Akademic Abraham is based. (The same ship I was on trips to the High Arctic and Antarctica.) We then went through the old part of the city that still has the old German villas. I was told by Katarina that many rich Russians are buying the villas from the occupants and restoring them. She referred to them as robbers and crooks since that is how many have made their money. Katarina usually serves as an interpreter at another oceanography institute and has been on several voyages on the Akademic Abraham, even once to the port of Boston. She spoke about the major castle that was partly destroyed in the war. After the war, Stalin ordered it destroyed to rid the city of German reminders and to make it a Russian city. (East Prussia had been part of Germany for six hundred years.) All Germans there after the war were sent back to Germany.

Today many Germans come back to see their childhood homes and to talk with the present owners. (Indeed, many were staying at my hotel.) I was told that many Germans are doing a lot of business investment in Kaliningrad. My host kept debating what will happen to the area since it is German, but only Russians live there. Most of the Russians have never been out of Kaliningrad since it takes two visas to go to the big Russia and return, and ship travel is slow and planes expensive. Katarina thinks it may someday become part of Poland or Lithuania with only a Russian port. She was born Russian in Lithuania. The Russians started to build a big Russian-style building at the castle site but ran out of money to finish it. They restored the damaged cathedral (also bombed by the British), and the authorities agreed to do so because many famous people are buried at the cathedral. We also visited part of the inner fortress, where there is an artificial lake and restaurant.

On Saturday, I had a bad night; the room was new and nice but no air-conditioning. So I opened the window to cool off, but the traffic noise was bad, and mosquitoes came in. Later, I was awoken by a beautiful fireworks display. I had also missed out on dinner as the hotel restaurant had a private party going on, and the bar was not serving any food. I went out and bought a bag of chips and two soft drinks. Before breakfast the next morning, I took an hour walk. It was nice to see the city with less activity. The breakfast was great, and I heard a lot of German. There were also many Russian athletes in the city for a sports competition; one lady told me all types of sports. Later, my driver came and took me to the airport. Check-in was very confusing, but somehow I

managed to get to my gate without announcements
or signs. For boarding, my fellow passengers and I
had to walk across the airport taxing area to our
plane. There, we had to wait about fifteen minutes at
the bottom of the plane stairway prior to boarding.
During the wait, a couple of small boys walked over
to a grass area next to the runway to pee. People
were still coming on board forty-five minutes later.
The flight left about noon. I was pleased that the
air-conditioning was on since it was very warm at
the airport. The one-and-a-half-hour flight was full
of Russians unlike my flight from Moscow.

We landed at the Sheremetyevo airport, north
of Moscow. Tomorrow I leave from the other major
airport in the south of Moscow. In going by taxi to
the airport the next day, I was reminded of the large
number of foreign cars, especially Japanese, in the
crowded streets, with bad traffic. Twenty years ago,
there were only Ladas on the streets and only a few
of them with no traffic jams. Now there are lots of
new shops, with colorful signs on the buildings, and
they even have the tallest building in Europe, an
apartment building.

II

Following their midmorning arrival in Moscow, the Czermaks
took a taxi to the Rossiya Hotel. Following check-in, they had
a hard time finding their room in the largest hotel in Europe.
After unpacking, they went to the hotel restaurant for a leisurely
lunch, followed by a long walk near the area of the hotel. They
spent some time at several souvenir shops before returning to
the hotel for an early dinner.

After a long dinner, they went to their room, where Deborah says, "James, I am tired and will bathe and then go to bed."

"Well, I am wide awake, so as you bathe, I will go out for a short walk to see what the area around the hotel looks like at night. On my return, I will take a shower and join you in bed, dear wife."

James takes a short walk near the hotel in an area where no one is about. At one point, he hears a car coming behind him. He turns around to see a fast-moving car, with its headlights off, coming down the sidewalk at him. Immediately, he jumps into a doorway as the car speeds by. He recognizes the driver as the same person who started the fire in his laboratory months ago.

James returns to the hotel very shaken up. After entering their room, James tells Deborah with nervous words what had happened. She jumps out of bed and gives him a hug. "James, I am so sorry and scared. What can we do?"

"I am also frightened and do not know what to do. Should I report this to the police and start being incredibly careful during our visit here? Maybe I will just ask Misha in the morning what he thinks I should do. He is the general secretary of the Russian Academy of Sciences and has many connections to people in high places. Meanwhile, we must be careful not to let anyone enter the room. I will put a chair against the door and make sure it is double locked in addition to the chain being hooked."

In the morning, Misha and Sonya join the Czermaks for breakfast in the hotel. Over their meal, James tells Misha about the attempt on his life the night before and asks his advice on what he should do.

"Well, John, if you do not know this man's name, I think it's wise not to bring the police into the matter but to do your best to be very careful. You will be in the hotel during the conference, with many colleagues around, so there should be no worries here. My driver Alexander, Sonya, and I will be with you both anytime you plan to go out of the hotel. Just phone me. On the tour of Moscow, midway through the conference, you both will be with many of our friends and their wives on the tour bus, so certainly, you will also be okay that day. Of course, we will take you to the airport following the five-day conference."

After their meal, Deborah suggests to James, "Perhaps you should consider starting to use your first name since everyone here at the conference knows you as John."

"That's an excellent idea. At Clemson, I started using James instead of John. In Chile, since I did not know my name, Deborah suggested I use her late husband's name, Richard. Before I became a teenager, my folks called me Johnny!"

Everyone laughs as John agrees to a name change.

Following their meal, John and Misha go to the hotel auditorium for the start of the conference that includes John presenting the plenary lecture. Alexander comes to the hotel and escorts Sonya and Deborah to the Academy of Sciences' car for a drive around Moscow in heavy traffic. The traffic was so bad in one place that Alexander drove down a sidewalk for half a block to get around a lane of stopped cars. They finally arrived at Tamara's university, followed by a lengthy lunch at her home.

During the lunch, Sonya tells Deborah about her university during USSR times. "In the toilets, we called them Happy Rooms where there was no toilet paper. Everyone had to use pieces of newspaper. We did not have computers either. Now we have toilet paper and computers."

After spending most of the afternoon in Sonya's apartment, they both return to the hotel by taxi to freshen up before the conference welcome reception.

John and Misha left the afternoon sessions early so Misha could show John around the Academy of Sciences that is in an old palace. "Misha, you certainly have a lovely corner office with a wonderful view of the park. Could you please take a photo of me with the nice painting of Mendeleev in the meeting room? Here is my camera."

"Now smile for the picture. This room is where the academy leaders meet and electronically bring in the far east, Ural, and other divisions. Let us go over to the Academy of Sciences high rise and take the elevator to the twenty-fourth floor, where you can take some good pictures of the city."

Misha went back to work about four, and Alexander drove John back to the hotel.

The evening reception was held in the hotel's ballroom with most of the conference attendees, and some with their wives, attending. There was plenty of food and drinks served buffet style, and John had numerous reunions with old friends, including Dmitri and Oleg, coauthors with John on a series of books they wrote for the IAEA. Deborah got to meet some of John's friends and their wives, and spent most of the time talking with some of the wives who knew English.

The next day, the conference resumed while Deborah stayed in the hotel to rest and do some reading. She joined John for the conference lunch, where they discussed their activities of the morning. "I had a leisurely stay in the room not doing a lot, just watching a little television and reading more of your diary. How is the conference going?"

"Well, it's nice to see some friends and hear about their research, but to be honest, the science does not interest me very much these days. I would rather be hearing talks about trips to faraway places. Tomorrow should be interesting for you since we will take the conference tour. Our bus driver and tour guide are supposed to show us the city's iconic sights. Our group will spend a lot of time walking around Red Square, followed by visiting St. Basil's Cathedral, the Armory Museum, and Novodevichy Convent. Following lunch, we will visit the Memorial Museum of Astronautics and the Monument to the Conquerors of Space. The day will conclude with dinner at the Rossiya restaurant. Misha and Sonya will both be working at their institutes tomorrow, but we will see them tonight at their apartment."

"That all sounds wonderful. I am excited about the tour."

"Well, I should return to the conference. What are your plans before dinner?"

"I will go for a walk and do some window-shopping."

"Well, sweetheart, please be careful. Remember, there is a murderer in the city that wants me dead, and he may want to use you to get to me."

After being picked up in the evening by Alexander, the three arrive at the apartment late because of traffic jams. At the party, there are several mutual friends of both Misha and John and their wives. The small group had a great time talking about old times over a delicious meal that Sonya had fixed. Later, the Czermaks thanked their hosts and said their goodbyes to the other guests since Alexander needed to leave.

The next evening following the tour and dinner at the hotel, Deborah tells John, "Sonya will take me shopping tomorrow, followed by more sightseeing. I assume you will listen to lectures all day. By the way, who do you usually sit next to at the conferences lunches?"

"Beautiful Svetlana on one side of me and gorgeous Katarina on the other side. Just kidding! It is always my dear friends Misha, Oleg, and Dmitri. As you know, we can eat all we want from the buffet with a large variety of food. I especially like the borscht soup."

"John, after our return from Europe, what are your plans for us?"

"Yes, now is a good time to start our plans for spending the rest of our lives happily together. My desire is to return to Clemson and put my two homes up for sale. After both are sold, we can move to Nederland. Perhaps we can live at your place to get away from the snow in Colorado for a couple of months each year. But of course, I want to teach you to ski. What do you think of my crazy plan?"

"Living in Colorado sounds great. I am not sure I want to keep my home. Perhaps we can decide later if I should sell or not. I know if we keep it, Eduardo and Maria will look after it when we are not there."

"After our return to Europe this weekend, we will have plenty of time to decide our future. Now it's bedtime."

After breakfast the next morning, John returns to the conference, and Alexander and Sonya pick up Deborah for more sightseeing and shopping.

In the evening, Alexander and the Czermaks go to a fancy restaurant for dinner. Dmitri and Oleg and their wives join the three. After they order their meals, Oleg asks John, "What do you think of the conference?"

"It has certainly been nice to spend some time with you all and to have some reunions with other friends I have not seen in several years. Most of the papers were interesting."

Dmitri comments, "Your lecture was first class, and it was great to hear about your students' research. What are your plans after you both leave Moscow?"

Deborah speaks up. "We will first return to Vienna for a couple of days then take the train around Austria followed by going to Prague to see John's favorite city. We will end the trip with a visit to Warsaw, and perhaps Gdansk, then home."

John tells the group that since he is retired now, he and Deborah will do more traveling. "By the way, I plan to play hooky tomorrow and skip the morning papers so I can sleep in and catch up on some writing in my diary."

The conversations continued as everyone ate their tasty food. The party ended with Dmitri and Oleg and their wives departing and the other three going to the academy car for their travels to the hotel.

Both John and Deborah were late in waking from a long night's sleep and skipped breakfast. However, they went for an early lunch before the morning session of lectures ended. Later, John returned to the conference room to hear the last few papers and participate in a discussion period for the attendees to comment on the papers. Deborah had gone to their room to pack, watch television, and get ready for the evening.

The farewell banquet was first class with plenty of delicious food and lots of drinking and dancing. After the joyous dinner and telling their friends goodbye, the Czermaks return to their room. John urgently goes to the bathroom. A minute later, there is a knock on the door. Without thinking, Deborah opens the door and is pushed back by an intruder holding a gun. Deborah lets out a scream as the guy slams the door shut. John comes charging out of the bathroom and is shocked by what he sees.

The intruder says, "My name is Nikolai Pushkin, son of Andrei Pushkin and elder brother of Alex. You killed them both, Czermak! I know that you killed my father from what Alex told me on his short visit to Moscow following our father's death. I found out about your survival in Chile and you being charged for killing my brother from reading the story about you and Alex in *Pravda*, the main Russian newspaper. Before your arrival in Moscow, *Pravda* also had a story about the conference being held at the Rossiya Hotel and that you were the keynote speaker. I assumed you would be staying here and stalked you to discover you taking a walk near the hotel the first night you arrived. I am sorry I did not kill you that night. I was also the one that tried to murder you in your car during my short visit to South Carolina. I am sorry that I accidentally killed your wife and sorrier you did not die in the fire I set in your laboratory. It was easy to break into the building and turn off the water to the fire sprinkler system.

"My uncle wanted to help me kill you tonight, but I told him I did not need his assistance. I regret that I have to kill your friend first, but she is a witness."

Nikolai then shoots Deborah in the chest, and John cries out, "No!"

He then turns the gun on John and shoots, but John, wounded in the chest, manages to lunge at Nikolai and puts him in a bear hug, trying to wrestle the gun from him. Then the gun goes off a third time, and the bullet goes through Nikolai's heart. The couple in the next room hears the shots and calls the front desk. After phoning the police, the clerk comes and unlocks the door with his master key. The couple and the clerk discover the three bodies and try to stop the bleeding with towels. Ten minutes later, an ambulance and police arrive, and the medical technicians manage to stop the Czermaks bleeding and take them to a nearby hospital. Following a police investigation of the murder scene, Nikolai is transported to the morgue.

After the wounded Czermaks are treated in the hospital's emergency room, John is taken to a recovery room and Deborah to the morgue. She did not survive the shot to her chest. John's wound was below his heart, and he will recover.

Epilogue

A few days later, as John is continuing to recover in the hospital, he receives a visit from Misha, Oleg, and Dmitri. John tells them both the whole story of the attempts on his life in California, Antarctica, South Carolina, and Moscow. "My biggest regret is that my three wives were murdered on my account. I am not sure I can go on living a normal life with the guilt."

Misha asks, "Do you have any concern that Andrei's brother might make an attempt on your life?"

"I don't know. I am being discharged the day after tomorrow and will make arrangements for my return to the U.S. with Deborah's body so she can have a proper burial at our home in Colorado. I will also have memorials for her in Boulder and on Navarino Island in Chile. I will be careful during these days for the brother's revenge, even though I do not know what he looks like."

Misha says, "John, if there is anything we can do to help you, please let us know. I would be happy to take you to the hotel and, later, the airport."

"Thank you, and I really appreciate you all coming here to visit me."

During the last night in the hospital, a man quietly enters John's room and starts to suffocate him with a pillow. He says, "This is for you killing my brother and two nephews." Although John is very weak, he tries to fight off the intruder but soon passes out. At the same time, a nurse enters the room and screams. The man pushes her aside and runs from the room and out of the hospital. The nurse then calls for help as she is administering CPR to the lifeless man.

Acknowledgments

I thank my late wife, Sylvia Tascher, for assisting me telepathically from heaven in my writing of *The Third Bear Hug*.

About the Author

Dr. James D. Navratil was educated as an analytical chemist at the University of Colorado and is now professor emeritus of environmental engineering and earth sciences at Clemson University in South Carolina. His other teaching experiences include serving as a chemical training officer in the U.S. Army Reserve, teaching general chemistry at the University of Colorado, and teaching chemical engineering and extractive metallurgy subjects at the University of New South Wales, Australia, where he also served as head of the Department of Mineral Processing and Extractive Metallurgy. In addition, he was an affiliate professor at the Colorado School of Mines, University of Idaho, and Clemson University as well as a visiting professor at the Technical University in Prague.

Dr. Navratil's industrial experience was acquired primarily at the U.S. Department of Energy (DOE), Rocky Flats Plant (RFP), and through his assignments with the International Atomic Energy Agency (IAEA), Chemical Waste Management, DOE's Energy Technology Engineering Center, Idaho National Engineering and Environmental Laboratory, Rust Federal Services, and Hazen Research, Inc.

Dr. Navratil earned numerous honors, including a Dow Chemical Scholarship, the annual award of the Colorado Section of the American Chemical Society (ACS), Rockwell International Engineer of the Year, two IR-100 awards, and three society fellowships. He was a member of the IAEA team awarded the 2005 Nobel Peace Prize and, in 2006, received the Lifetime Achievement Award for Commitment to the Waste-Management, Education and Research Consortium (WERC) and to WERC's International Environmental Design Contests.

Dr. Navratil has four patents to his credit and has given more than 450 presentations, including lectures in more than one hundred countries. He has coedited or coauthored 19 books (most recently with Fedor Macasek, *Separations Chemistry*, and with Jiri Hala, *Radioactivity, Ionizing Radiation, and Nuclear Energy*), published more than 250 scientific publications, and served on the editorial boards of over a dozen journals. He was instrumental in the founding of the journals *Solvent Extraction and Ion Exchange* (serving as coeditor for many years) and *Preparative Chromatography* (serving as editor) as well as the ACS's Subdivision of Separation Science and Technology (SST) and its award in SST and DOE's Actinide Separation Conferences and its Glenn Seaborg Award in Actinide Separations. Dr. Navratil has also organized or co-organized many conferences, symposiums, and meetings for the ACS, DOE, and IAEA.

He is a diamond member of the Traveler's Century Club (www.travelerscenturyclub.org) having visited 307 countries and territories on the club list of 327. Some of these travels are described herein.

Summary

The Third Bear Hug is a continuation of the stories in *The Bear Hug* and *The Final Bear Hug*. The story begins in the later book with John James Czermak and his wife, Margrit, returning to their home in Arvada, Colorado, after spending almost three years in Vienna, Austria, where John worked for the International Atomic Energy Agency (IAEA). John is a world-renowned nuclear scientist and contributor to the development of the neutron bomb and returns to his job as manager of Plutonium Chemistry Research and Development at the Rocky Flats Plant near Denver Colorado, where triggers for nuclear weapons are made. In Vienna, Margrit was romantically involved with Andrei Pushkin, thought by the CIA to be a KGB agent. Realizing the futility of their relationship, Andrei and Margrit had on several occasions unsuccessfully attempted to terminate it. But Andrei suffered continual agonizing self-debasement and eventually left Vienna for Canada after faking his suicide.

Following their return to Colorado, John and Margrit resume a close, loving relationship that had been severely damaged in Vienna. About this time, John is recruited by Tim Smith of the CIA to see if some countries have a secret nuclear weapon program under way. It was easy for John to collect intelligence information for Tim since he traveled to conferences around the world and to Vienna and Moscow to have meetings with his Russian coauthors on a series of books they were writing for the IAEA. Following more contacts with his Russian colleagues, John was informed that a background investigation had been conducted by the Department of Energy and the FBI. This investigation resulted in John losing his security clearance.

John was then granted a three-year leave of absence to teach in Australia. Tim kept in contact with John and requested him to visit certain countries and find out if they might be producing nuclear weapons. During his travels, there were several attempts on his life. After his return from his leave of absence, he starts work in California. There, Andrei surprisingly contacts Margrit, trying to renew their love affair. Margrit rejects him since she has a good relationship with John and tells Andrei she might go with him if she was a divorcée or widow. This statement prompts Andrei to try and kill John, but instead, he accidentally kills Margrit. Upon hearing the news of her death, Andrei commits suicide and tells his son Alex in his dying breath that John had shot him and wants Alex to kill John.

Czermak wants to start a new life and leaves California for a teaching job at Clemson University in South Carolina and even starts using his middle name, James. Andrei's son Alex joins James's research group using a different last name. Ying from China also joins his group, and a loving relationship develops between the two. The story in *The Final Bear Hug* concludes during an expedition in Antarctica that Tim supports to see if one of the Russian crew members is passing nuclear weapon's information to a group of Argentinian scientists.

On the expedition, James and Ying are married by the captain, and Alex tries to kill James but later finds out that James did not kill his father. On the last night of the voyage, during a violent rainstorm, Alex meets James at the stern of the ship and makes amends to him, which ends by Alex giving James a big bear hug that causes both of them to accidentally fall into the rough and freezing ocean.

The story in *The Third Bear Hug* begins on the morning following the violent storm. A man and two ladies discover James washed up on the shore of Cape Horn. They take him back by fishing boat to Deborah's home on another island. The couple is Deborah's neighbors, and she is a retired medical doctor. She assists James in recovering but finds out he has amnesia and does not remember anything prior to being washed up on land. Deborah agrees to let James help her around her small farm. Several months later, the two start to travel to different parts of Chile, and a loving relationship develops. James's memory slowly returns after an accidental meeting with a friend in Peru and returns to Clemson to have a reunion with Ying, family, and friends. The university appoints James as chairman of the chemistry department. During this time, Ying gets killed in a hit-and-run accident that was meant for James. A week later, another attempt is made on James's life in his university laboratory, but he manages to escape the Molotov cocktail fire.

James is then contacted by CIA Agent Kim Carn, who requests him to go on certain trips to collect intelligence for the CIA. The last technical conference James attends is in Moscow, and he asks Deborah to accompany him. On the trip, they spend a few days in Vienna, where they get married. The Czermaks then go onto Moscow so James can attend the conference. On the last night of the meeting, the two are confronted in their hotel room by a man with a gun who identifies himself as Nikolai Pushkin, Andrei's son and Alex's elder brother. Before he shoots Deborah and then James, he says, "This is for killing my father and brother." Gravely wounded, James jumps over and gives Nikolai a bear hug, trying to wrestle the gun from him, but it goes off putting a bullet into Nikolai's heart, killing him.

The story concludes with Deborah dying and James recovering. However, Andrei's brother, Alexei, is determined to kill James since he is convinced that James was responsible for the deaths of his brother and two nephews.

Author's note: You may find out if Alexei is successful in killing Prof. John James Czermak when you read this book. Globe-trotters will especially enjoy reading about some of the author's travels.